Why I Love My Gay Boyfriend

Sabrina Zollo

central avenue publishing

2012

Central Avenue Publishing Edition

This Central Avenue Publishing edition is published by arrangement with Sabrina Zollo.

www.centralavenuepublishing.com

First print edition published by Central Avenue Publishing,
an imprint of Central Avenue Marketing Ltd.

WHY I LOVE MY GAY BOYFRIEND

ISBN 978-1-926760-89-6

Published in Canada with international distribution.

Cover Design: Michelle Halket

Author Photo: Pokin Yeung

Cover Illustrations: Courtesy & Copyright CanStock Photo: lindwa; blamb; kariiika

Dedicated to my parents, Crescencia and Tancredi Zollo,
for their unconditional love and support.

Despite all their wisdom, they still think I'm awesome.

Why I Love My Gay Boyfriend

Chapter 1: Dishonourable

My decision to accept a job at Gisele, a global cosmetics empire, was easy. Lack of options and desperation lead to swift decision-making.

After my first week of work, my three best friends took me out to our favourite pub, The Betty Ford Clinic, as consolation, rather than celebration. While settling didn't deserve a fist bump, it certainly served as a valid reason to drink excessively.

"Cheers to selling your soul!" A mixture of beer bottles and glasses clinked together in honour of my future at Gisele.

"Hopefully I'll just be selling makeup and not any souls," I replied after taking a generous sip of my gin and tonic.

"Gisele is a great resume builder," Calista said to offset Jackie's charming proclamation of the demise of my soul. Calista is doing her PhD in Economics and will soon rule the world. She is brilliant and the sweetest person I know, after my mom. "Two years at Gisele and Amnesty International will be begging you to come work for them."

Amnesty International was my first and only choice after graduating with an MBA. Gisele was on my Top 5, as in *Top 5 companies I would only consider if desperate.*

"I expect a *lot* of free makeup." It never fails to surprise me how successful Jackie is at getting what she wants just by asking for it. The one thing that she never has to ask for is a date. She has dated and dumped half of Toronto. Life is good for Jackie. "And I can teach you how to put it on," she offered.

"I think it's so funny that you got this job and you never wear make-up." Lindsay, my most practical friend, never wears makeup either. She works in environmental management for the city but isn't the granola tree-hugging type. She's refreshingly down to earth and still believes in true love.

In my eyes, my three best friends, Jackie, Calista and Lindsay, were wise old souls. They had been building their careers and lives for the past two years while I was trying to figure out my life's calling at grad school. The frustrating thing about a life's calling is that it's not prone to fall into one's lap. A life's calling should not be playing hard to get.

"So what are the people like?" Lindsay asked.

"I don't know why, but they all hate me. How could they hate me so much before they even know me?" This bothered me more than I liked to admit. I was still young and naïve enough to believe that my self-worth was determined by my popularity. "There's also something very strange about them. I don't know, maybe I'm being too harsh but they seem almost…dishonourable. I don't trust them."

"But most importantly, is your boss hot?" Jackie interjected.

"What makes you think they're dishonourable? I mean, other than the fact that they hate you, of course." Calista asked, as we all ignored Jackie's question.

"Well…" I paused to search for a positive spin but couldn't find one. "It's like they don't have any morals or human decency."

That began my dramatic description of my experience at Gisele, as I tried to capture the horror of my first day:

Gisele occupied the top floor of an imposing thirty-seven storey office building in the heart of Toronto's trendy Yorkville. The Gisele office was designed to awe and intimidate. As the elevator doors opened on Gisele's vast two-story lobby, I was greeted with what felt like a corporate glacier. The air felt icy and thin. The landscape was composed of towering mirrored walls, an expansive reception desk made of carrera marble, white limestone floors and white leather Barcelona chairs. If hell were frozen, it just might look like this.

Life-size backlit Gisele print advertising lined the walls like modern day gargoyles. The eyes of the skinny models followed me as I entered the lobby. They looked empty and hungry. As I walked towards the reception desk, the models seemed poised to leap out of the frame and devour me. At night this would be a scary place. An enormous HD television was mounted behind the desk, looping Gisele television ads with no sound. It was as if the models were trapped in the television like a bad dream in which you tried to scream and no sound came out.

My boss Savannah, a Marketing Director at Gisele, was away on a business trip, so my co-worker Heidi was charged with giving me a tour of the office and introducing me to my colleagues. I asked the disinterested receptionist for Heidi, who kept me waiting uncomfortably in the wintry lobby for twenty minutes. I heard the piercing sound of high heel stilettos punctuating the cold floor before I saw Heidi.

Heidi was a skinny, pretty girl who wore too much makeup and was dressed for Paris Fashion Week. Everything about her appearance was in excess, and a little inappropriate for daytime, from her Farrah waves to her smoky eye make-up. I knew she could not afford her outfit and Christian Louboutin shoes on our salary and speculated whether she moonlit as a high-end escort.

"Veronica?" She shamelessly looked me up and down. Twice. I wondered if it was her high-heels or my outfit from H&M that was making her grimace in pain. I could tell she hated me instantly.

"Yes, hi!" I said, attempting to be friendly, jumping up abruptly and holding out my hand for a handshake.

"I'm Heidi, the Assistant Brand Manager for Gisele, Lip & Nail." She gingerly shook my hand. She had long, fake nails that were painted black. "Follow me."

Heidi led me through the glass doors to the eerily quiet office and into a maze of generic, clinical-looking cubicles. It seemed like we were in the belly of the whale, where entry-level employees were swallowed whole, miles away from any natural light and any means of escape.

As we encountered the victims of the corporate whale, it was somewhat of a consolation that the head-to-toe inspection was part of Heidi's routine.

"Hi, how are you?" Down. Up

"Good, how are you?" Down. Up.

"Good."

Heidi robotically repeated this exchange with everyone we encountered along the way, perhaps as a means of demonstrating her self-proclaimed popularity. The exchange seemed disingenuous as it was clear from their body language that neither party liked each other. The Heidi Inspection would end with a smug smile. She reminded me of a smiling shark.

Heidi did not bother to introduce me to anyone we passed. I suspected she was strictly and grudgingly following instructions to introduce me to my immediate co-workers. Beyond that, she did not feel it worthwhile to make me feel welcome. My first introductions were to Heidi's BFFs, Jasmine and Chloe.

Heidi stopped abruptly in front of a glass-paneled cube. "Jasmine, this is Veronica."

Jasmine was seated in her cube with her back as straight as a concrete slab. It was like she was so fiercely proud that she refused any support – even back support. She had a stern-looking face that seemed incapable of smiling. Her dark hair was pulled back in a chignon that was so tight it looked angry. As she stood up to shake my hand, her chin jutted slightly forward so that she could look down at me even though she was only five foot two. Despite her small frame, she was intimidating.

"Hello, Veronica. I am Jasmine Petite." She pronounced her last name quickly and with a strong, French accent, so that it sounded like "tit" to the unsophisticated ear, such as mine.

"Hi, Jasmine... *Tit*?" I repeated to make sure I heard correctly.

"No," she replied haughtily, "It is *Pe-tite*." She enunciated the word slowly. "It is French for small. I am from France. I moved to Canada for my boyfriend." She added the last disclaimer as if it were the only plausible reason anyone would move to Canada.

Jasmine was fluent in English but over-pronounced her words like Madonna does trying to sound British, as if every word she uttered were a revelation. Unfortunately for her, she would always be Jasmine Tit to me.

"Oh. People must have trouble pronouncing your last name," I said in a gesture of sympathy.

"No," she lied. "Just you."

Yup, she hated me too. I wondered what was wrong with me. Did I smell bad? I tried to remember whether I put on deodorant that morning.

Next up was Chloe, the Assistant Brand Manager for GiGi, the edgier, lifestyle brand of Gisele. In fact, everything was edgy about Chloe: her demeanor; her angular face; her asymmetrical bob hairstyle and her bony frame. It was also hate at first sight for Chloe.

Heidi introduced to me to Chloe. "Chloe, you'll need to add Veronica to The Tracker."

"OK, what's your story?" Chloe asked as she opened a spreadsheet on her computer and promptly began interrogating me.

My background volunteering as a Marketing Coordinator for the Sierra Club grabbed Chloe's attention. "Charity work? Why the hell do you want to work here?"

"Uh, it's a great opportunity." It was a weak response and did not appear to convince her.

"OK, I'm putting you down last on The Tracker," was Chloe's swift decision.

"What is The Tracker?" I ventured to ask.

"It's a list of all the Assistant Brand Managers, their internal and external work experience and their performance rating, listed in descending order of estimated promotion," Chloe explained.

"How did you get all that information?"

"Chloe knows everything and everyone," Heidi replied in solidarity of The Tracker.

"The Tracker has never been wrong," Chloe affirmed.

I looked at the seventeen or so names listed before me. Chloe was first, followed by Heidi and Jasmine. "Well, I have a long way to go," I joked. There was a tense silence. So far, no friends yet.

Heidi then introduced me to Matt, one of the only heterosexual men who worked at Gisele. He was a good-looking guy until he opened his mouth. It became immediately clear that Matt joined Gisele to pick up hot chicks. He figured his chances were good in a company full of beauty-obsessed women and gay men. Matt had Hot Chick ADD and couldn't talk to you without wandering eyes lest he miss any sight of tits or ass. Quantity, not quality, was his objective. He had more testosterone than I believed to be normal. After speaking to him I felt like taking a bath in Purell.

"Hi, I'm Veronica Lopez," I introduced myself.

"I'm Matt, but you, Miss Lopez, can call me Mateo." He did not appear to possess a drop of Latino blood.

"Um, OK."

"So, Savannah's your boss?" Mateo asked. "I hear she's psychotic."

"Actually, she seems pretty cool," I replied from what I recalled from our coffee chat after I landed the job.

"I love crazy chicks too but I wouldn't work for one," he grinned.

"That's not what I meant," I said, almost recoiling with my growing disgust for him.

"Well if you ever need any advice, you know where to find me," he offered with a slimy wink.

"Uh, I won't need any help, thanks."

"Savannah is very fashion-forward...for an older woman," Heidi said to us on a completely unrelated note before she led me to Sydney's cube. Based on my guesstimate, Savannah was in her early thirties, and hardly classified as an "older" woman.

"Sydney's a slack-off." Heidi warned me as we approached Sydney's cube.

"We all work our asses off and Sydney has figured out a way to leave by five o'clock everyday and not get fired." I got the impression it was not the first time Heidi had shared her highly esteemed opinion of Sydney.

"I'm in a cube, I can hear you," Sydney said. She swiveled in her chair to face us. Sydney was a tall redhead with a perfectly pale complexion and piercing blue eyes. She seemed unaffected by Heidi's rant. In fact, it seemed that not much would rattle her steely disposition.

"This is Veronica. She's new but they haven't figured out where to put her," Heidi said.

"Hi Veronica. I'm Sydney. By the way, the work day ends at five so that's when we're supposed to leave."

"If you want to get ahead at Gisele, you have to work crazy hours." Heidi corrected Sydney.

Calista interrupted my story, jolting me out of my dramatic rendition and back to the comforting reality of the pub. "It sounds like Heidi is giving you good advice, even though it's probably not what you wanted to hear."

"Yeah, and Sydney doesn't seem that bad." Lindsay's optimism had apparently taken over her judgment.

"No, she's a bitch too." I clarified.

"Because she hates you, too? That doesn't make her a bitch, it just means she has bad taste in people." Jackie said in support of my congeniality.

"How's your boss?" Lindsay asked.

"I'll let you know about that when she's back from New York. I've been warned about her by more people than just Mateo."

"Don't let people psych you out," Calista advised.

"Maybe they're threatened by you because you're different," Lindsay suggested.

"I'm not *that* intimidating," I laughed.

"Maybe they judged you as quickly as you judged them," Calista added. "Give them a chance. Try being more open-minded."

"For example," Jackie said, "I came here with an open mind and I see a lot of good things. Is it just me or are there a lot of hot guys here tonight?"

"I'll drink to that!" I raised my fourth glass of gin and tonic in honour of hot guys. "Calista, I will accept your challenge, because you are a wise Yoda Zen master. However, I'm pretty sure it's a lost cause."

"So do you want to lay a wager on how long it takes Veronica before she turns into a bitch too?" Jackie joked.

"On her fourth glass of gin and tonic!" Lindsay laughed – pointing at my three empty glasses.

"I'm a lovely drunk!" I protested.

Chapter 2: Dream in a Bottle

SO HOW DID I END up in this unlikely conundrum in the first place? I was beginning the second year of my MBA when I stumbled across Gisele at my university's fall recruitment fair. I was completing my double major in non-profit organization and marketing and had high hopes of working for a respected global non-profit organization such as Amnesty International.

I had had very little sleep the night before because my boyfriend had predictably broken up with me. I say predictably because according to Calista, I'm attracted to men who are emotionally unavailable, or, as I like to refer to them in retrospect: douche bags. I had stayed up all night begging my latest douche bag to reconsider, stripping myself of any self-respect in a display of desperation that set the women's movement back seventy years. Needless to say, this was not an effective strategy in retaining any man, let alone a douche bag. Thus, that day I was *sans* douche bag and not feeling particularly fresh.

I was not inspired to put on a power suit and my best game face to show recruiters my eagerness to slave away the best years of my life. You spend your MBA bonding with your peers in team-based projects (i.e., pulling last minute all-nighters) and social events (i.e., drinking games at the campus pub) only to be pitted against one another in competition over the few promising jobs available during campus recruitment. As I entered the recruitment battleground, my new frienemies were nodding emphatically, smiling toothily and vigorously shaking hands. I could imagine what they were saying:

"Yes, I would definitely stab my friend in the back for the promotion! I'm so career-driven and ambitious that the only friends I have are people that I can use to further my career! I'm completely shameless and transparent!"

"I would *absolutely* risk divorce by prioritizing my career over my husband and delaying childbirth until all my eggs rot!"

"Hi, I spent my MBA partying incessantly because I knew I would have to give up any notion of a personal life once I started working for you! Don't worry I don't need any sleep. I've learned to survive on Red Bull and coke... ha, ha Coca Cola, that is!"

At least seventy companies across several sectors (consumer packaged goods, banking, accounting, consulting) had booths set up, espousing corporate rah-rah and scouting top talent. I was on the lookout for not-for-profit companies when I approached the Gisele booth. It appeared that Gisele's Human Resources Manager had been trained to project the warmth of a cold, hard bitch because she was doing an exceptional job of it. Despite her smug look of superiority and disdain, she was being mauled by a clawing army of fashionable women and gay men.

I was inflicted with temporary post-break-up insanity – a combination of hyper denial and ADD. I stopped to make completely un-MBA inspired conversation with a short, chubby man standing at the outskirts of the Gisele booth. He reminded me a little bit of an Oompa Loompa from Charlie and the Chocolate Factory. However, I was in need of male attention and he appeared to be interested in my unorthodox approach.

"I may not know a lot about makeup, but I am a total skincare junkie," I admitted to him. "I don't know, something about the pretty little containers just makes me such a girl! You know?"

He nodded in agreement. "Beauty product packaging can be very exciting."

We intensely discussed the value of a toner at great length. "I wouldn't recommend it for dry skin," I advised him. "But if you have oily skin, the toner is instrumental in closing your pores. It is key to preventing blackheads and blemishes."

He was immensely impressed with my vast knowledge of facial skincare.

"Sell me this fragrance," he challenged me.

He handed me an elaborate pink bottle with a gold spritzer. I laughed. No amount of marketing prowess could get this short, fat man to buy this shit. He already had short man syndrome as it was. The last thing he needed was women's fragrance.

"This is not fragrance." He said dramatically and spritzed a pungent mist that I will forever associate with bullshit. He paused for effect. "It is a dream in a bottle."

"Wow."

As it were, not only did Oompa Loompa love the smell of bullshit, he was also the new VP of Human Resources transferred from the global head office to whip Gisele's Canadian office into shape. I also speculated that his appreciation for me extended to the fact that, having gained a Beyoncé-booty from my MBA diet of Kraft Dinner and Mr. Noodles, I now looked like a dirty librarian in my once well-fitting business suit.

"I want you to give your resume to Angela." He gestured to the cold hard bitch. "Tell her that I asked you to."

"Oh no, I'm not —" I began to clarify that I wasn't interested, but stopped myself. What did I have to lose? If anything, I could build up my interview experience and skills so I'd have the confidence to wow Amnesty International when they interview me. "I'm not quite ready to submit my resume yet. I'm still working on it."

"Here's my business card. E-mail me your resume later this week and I will arrange an interview."

The idea of dedicating my career to selling lipstick was as nauseating as the dream in a bottle that he had just spritzed all over me.

"One last very important question." He said as I took his card.

The next few words sent a shiver of excitement down my spine. "Paris or New York?"

"Pardon me?"

"Where would you rather work? Paris or New York?"

"I thought the job was here in Toronto?" I was visibly flabbergasted. New York? When does a Canadian business grad get the opportunity to transfer to New York straight out of business school with no work experience?

"It is, but within two years you can transfer to Paris or New York if you wish." He smiled, deducing from my reaction that he had hit the bull's eye.

"New York!" I exclaimed, feeling my cheeks flush with excitement. The head office of Amnesty International was located in New York and if I could sell a dream in a bottle then I could definitely sell equal human rights!

A day after I emailed my resume to Oompa Loompa, I was granted an interview with Gisele. A week later, Gisele held on-campus interviews with the top candidates from my MBA program, and me. I figured my dirty librarian garb would not be as effective with a lady interviewer so I had thrown together a blouse and dress pants from my non-existent business wardrobe. I was feeling very underdressed and plain as I waited in the Career Centre lounge with the other interview hopefuls, who looked like a collection of CIA agents in their serious-looking black suits.

"Is that what you're wearing to your interview?" Heather, my new frienemy, asked. She was seated neatly in her CIA suit, immaculately groomed with a black leather folder in her lap.

"Yeah, why?"

"You have a big stain on the front of your blouse," she indicated. A white dried toothpaste mark was smeared across my stomach.

"Oh, shit!" I was about to run to the bathroom to scrub it off when a lady from the Career Centre came to fetch me for my interview. I didn't know why I was panicking; I didn't want the job anyway. I could just strategically hold my arm in front of my stomach for the whole interview. Problem solved!

My seventeen minute interview with Angela was a joke. She appeared completely disinterested in my answers as I awkwardly held my cramping arm over the toothpaste stain. I was prepared for the typical, run of the mill interview questions, such as what is your greatest weakness ("I'm a perfectionist!") and what is your 5-year plan ("It's my dream to work at your company for my whole career!").

"Name a personality type you can't stand," she asked, bored.

I wasn't prepared for this question so answered honestly. "I hate arrogant people. They assume they know everything and aren't willing to listen, learn from others, or improve themselves."

She laughed. "Encounter many arrogant people in your MBA?"

I blushed, realizing I had vented candidly instead of giving a tactful, proper interview answer.

"I agree." she said, losing a little bit of the cold bitch edge, just as I was starting to warm up to it. "If Gisele were a woman, what would she be like?"

I drew a complete blank. After what seemed like an agonizingly long pause, I started describing Jackie. "She is confident in herself, knows who she is, is comfortable in her skin. She is fashionable, wears current clothes that are timeless, not trendy. She goes out for drinks after work every night, dates a lot of men, but never past the third date. She has a lot of friends from different circles, but keeps only a few close friends. Red wine and her Blackberry are dear to her heart."

Angela appeared to be impressed, "Hmm. That's a very detailed description. It's like Gisele is a good friend of yours."

"Well, good brands are like good friends." I smiled back. Is it just me or does someone smell bull shit? Boo-ya! Take that dream in a bottle.

Angela called me back a week later offering me the job. The cold bitch was gone as she greeted me like a long, lost friend over the phone.

"Really?" I stalled. "Aren't I supposed to have a second round interview?"

"No, we go by the gut," she answered happily. They must have had indigestion if they wanted to hire me.

"I'm currently interviewing with other companies..." I lied. The Canadian Amnesty International office was small and was not hiring so I had applied to an Amnesty International USA Field Organizer position. While I was an avid member of Amnesty International, I did not have the qualifications. "How long do I have to get back to you?"

"We could give you one week," she said generously.

The Career Centre at my school did not cater to non-profit companies so I was on my own. One week wasn't a lot of time to scope out and approach non-profit companies. It didn't seem ethical but maybe I could accept the Gisele job as a back-up while I pounded the non-profit pavement. It was clear that I would have to build my volunteer and non-profit business experience to even be considered by Amnesty International USA.

I scoured what I considered to be the top Canadian charities to no avail. I called the Sick Kids Foundation, World Wildlife Fund, the Salvation Army and the Canadian Red Cross Society but all open positions required at least two years of business experience. As my deadline approached, the more I started to panic. Selling lipstick and bottled dreams was slowly turning into my reality.

It was on D-Day that Heather, the toothpaste spotter, asked me in one of our classes whether I had heard back from Gisele.

"They offered me the job about a week ago," I said as tactfully as possible, knowing that Heather had interviewed for the same position. In fact, she had interviewed for a number of desirable positions. Heather had been a top student her whole life. She interned at Unilever over the summer and had been networking with top tier consumer packaged goods companies for several months. Needless to say, she never had toothpaste stains on her shirts. But she could probably market the hell out of any toothpaste.

"Oh," she said, disappointed and in disbelief. She offered weak congratulations.

"Thanks for letting me know about the toothpaste stain," I said sympathetically before I realized that it sounded like I was rubbing it in that she lost out to someone with a stained shirt.

"I didn't know that you even wanted to work at Gisele. Aren't you majoring in non-profit organization?"

"And Marketing," I found myself saying defensively.

"Well, you know you just got the job because you're good looking," she said.

I was dumbfounded by her un-MBA-like accusation. Firstly, she was openly admitting I was better-looking than her and secondly, upon reflection, it was a ridiculously easy interview. I thought back to my dirty librarian business suit and my curious conversation with Oompa Loompa. Uh-oh…maybe she had a point.

"Ouch. Jealously doesn't become you," I replied.

"I'm not jealous. You should know what you're getting into." It did seem like she was referring to a dream in a bottle. "Gisele is a sweatshop. You don't strike me as the kind of person that would survive in that kind of environment. You should only accept the job if it's something that you really want. Something that you would give up your life for." If Heather wasn't willing to give up her life for it, she was at least willing to give up her dignity, as was evident right now.

"What makes you think that I don't want it?" I answered, getting increasingly defensive.

"I'm not saying this to psych you out," she said, reading my mind. "It's true. Ask anyone." And she turned on her perfect kitten heel and walked smartly out of class.

I shouldn't have let a jealous frienemy get to me but my already less than ideal back-up option was starting to crash and burn. I called Lindsay on my way home to give her a play-by-play.

"Have you heard about Gisele? Is it a sweatshop?" I demanded.

"I have no idea," she laughed. "It sounds like Heather is just jealous. I wouldn't worry about it. Why don't you ask to speak to someone from the company?"

"You're brilliant!" Brilliant, except that my deadline was today.

Faced with no other choice, I resigned myself to accepting the job at Gisele as a contingency plan while continuing my search for a non-profit company. Angela was thrilled with my decision and arranged a meeting with my Director-to-be, Savannah, who would give me more details on the role and responsibilities. On the positive side, Gisele's compensation was certainly intriguing to someone who had to pay off her MBA student debts. It was doubtful that any non-profit company in Canada could match it. I was torn. I felt guilty taking a job away from someone like Heather who wanted it and because I knew I was only using Gisele until I found something better.

"What's the worst that can happen?" Calista counseled. "So you work for a couple of years at Gisele, build your resume, diversify your experience, make good money, pay off your student loans. Seems like a pretty good deal. Develop strong business acumen and then transition into non-profit at a more senior level. Don't feel like you don't have a choice. Because right now, you have a job that most girls would kill for."

"You're right," I said automatically because Calista is always right. Then I actually thought about it and realized she was right. What's the worst that could happen?

Chapter 3: Fashion Victim

So, here I was, working for Gisele as a peon, trying to channel the sage advice of Calista and open my mind. If I had not yet resigned myself to being open-minded about my hateful co-workers, I had at least remained open-minded to the career opportunity. With the promise of transferring to New York in two years, I re-focused my energy into beauty business boot camp instead of resenting my colleagues. In my first two weeks, Heidi had given me a litany of business material to read, starting with Gisele's riveting Lip & Nail segment: business reviews and marketing plans from the past three years; the five year new product pipeline; and the past three years of research.

My boss Savannah, was still in meetings and TV advertising shoots in New York and Heidi warned me that I needed to be fully up to speed on the business by the time she returned or I would be 'punished'. I found it an ominously strange choice of words.

"What do you mean by 'punished'? It sounds a little…harsh." I dared to ask for clarification.

"You don't want to find out," Heidi cautioned. It did not seem that Gisele was what you would call a nurturing culture.

Fuelled by fear of punishment, my Lip & Nail immersion amounted to several hours of boredom alone in my cube, hundreds of dead trees, thousands of hours of marketing peon blood, sweat, and tears and more than I ever needed or cared to know about lips and nails. In fact, my opinion of lips and nails had now moved from indifference to slight nausea. Is it OK to resent the people you work with and your product within two weeks of starting a new job?

My brain hurt from trying to process the onslaught of new data and new people. Quite irritatingly, there was an abnormally high usage of acronyms and random French terms, since Gisele's head office was in Paris and everyone was pretentious. So, not only did I not yet understand what people were talking about, I also literally did not understand what they were saying. It's like they were speaking another language and I was a visible minority, trying to fit into a foreign culture where all the people were beautiful, well-dressed and evil.

My first impression of my colleagues had not changed in two weeks. In my limited interactions with them, they continued to demonstrate their disdain for me. Their behaviour represented several forms of moral destitution. Human decency seemed to be an uncommon disposition at Gisele and I yearned for companionship that would not lead me to hell. Self-righteousness could be lonely.

Heidi appeared at my cube straight off the cover of Vogue and dumped a PR report on my cube, requesting that I make photocopies for our boss's bosses without looking at me. I bit my tongue to prevent myself from reminding her that I was not her secretary and decided to humour her in a gesture of goodwill.

While making good use of my MBA education in the photocopy room, I rocked what I believed to be a boho-chic outfit. Sure, people were looking me up and down a little longer than usual, but they were just admiring my easy breezy Cover Girl style.

"Ronnie!" a very gay man approached me excitedly, "We haven't met yet. I'm Stevie. I'm the Assistant Brand Manager on Fragrances. So nice to meet you!"

I shook his smooth, well-groomed hand. Funny, he seemed genuinely pleased to meet me. "I'm Veronica. Nice to meet you too," I responded suspiciously and waited for Stevie to demonstrate some sort of amoral behaviour.

"I think it's great that you can look so pretty even when you're dressed so grungy!" He gushed.

"I'm dressed grungy?" I asked, betraying my disappointment.

Stevie's eyes widened upon realization of his inadvertent insult. And with a suppressed gasp and a not-so-suppressed giggle, he fled from the photocopy room in a flourish of this season's must-haves. I looked down at my un-ironed plaid shirt paired with a men's vest and harem pants tucked into salt-stained brown Uggs. With a sinking heart, I realized that easy breezy Cover Girl style would probably go over better in the Cover Girl offices.

I returned to Heidi's cube now painfully aware of my fashion victim status. Heidi and Jasmine Tit were deep in conversation. I stood at Heidi's cube with the copies she had requested awkwardly in arm, not wanting to interrupt my fashion superiors. Apparently people dressed in ugly clothes were invisible to Heidi and Jasmine Tit. They continued their conversation as if I didn't exist.

"Hi," I finally said a little too loudly. They both turned to look at me in contempt and then with incredulousness at my outfit.

"What happened to your outfit?" Heidi recoiled, as if in fear of catching bad fashion.

"How did they let you in dressed like that?" Jasmine Tit asked in confusion. "My boyfriend wouldn't dare let me leave the apartment if I were dressed like that."

"You're welcome." I dropped the copies on Heidi's desk and returned back to fashion victim exile in my cube.

Several hours later, wallowing in my bad fashion sense and trying to strategically plan my exit, Stevie stopped by my cube with a pile of fashion magazines. "Here, some more reading material. You might pick up some fashion tips. For example, Uggs – just don't."

"Thanks for rubbing salt in the wound," I said miserably.

"No, no, I come in peaceful fashion intervention." Stevie reassured me. "I'm sorry I upset you. But admitting you have a problem is the first step."

"I don't have a problem! *You* all think I have a problem. There are more important things in life than fashion…" Stevie looked dubious. "…like world peace." I offered weakly.

"Honey, I'm afraid that while you're in *this* world, you do have a problem. Heidi and her BFFs will not leave you in peace until you are their fashion equal. Let me take you out for dinner. I can give you some fashion pointers, such as less is more," he looked pointedly at my harem pants. "And you can fill me in on world peace."

"Where?" I asked hesitantly. Stevie's intentions seemed good. He could be my fashion fairy. He would likely help me burn my outfit.

"Somewhere expensive and fabulous…like your outfit," he winked.

And so on our first date we went for a liquid dinner at the Drake Hotel. On a school night the Drake tends to attract pretentious and aging wannabe socialites. Cougars with Botox faces and even more questionable fashion sense than my own and metro-sexual, ambiguously gay men spawned hours of conversation.

Maybe it was the martinis talking but I believed that Stevie could very well be my platonic soul mate. It was like he knew the inner workings of my being and could only bring out the most fabulous in me. As opposed to my ex-boyfriends who only contributed to my insecurities and neuroses. But alas, Stevie was never going to be my boyfriend. Or…could he? I mean, albeit a gay one? After all, what was stopping us from hanging out, sharing (lots of) drinks, dreaming about shoes and having him accessorize my outfits? It was love at first fashion mistake. I knew at that moment that I would never call him a douche bag.

"So other than dressing well, what else does it take to succeed at Gisele?" I asked Stevie through my chocola-tini goggles.

"There are three cardinal rules to get ahead at Gisele: (1) always dress for success; (2) if you don't know what you're doing or saying, just bull shit with confidence; and (3) don't get romantically involved with someone more senior than you."

"Hmmm, have those cardinal rules been validated?" Even in my punch-love drunkenness I did not believe that Stevie had cracked the code.

"Those that don't follow the cardinal rules have not lasted long," Stevie warned. "I have seen people at Gisele build their careers on bull shit. The truth is, no one knows what the hell they're talking about! The secret to success is that you can't let people know that *you* don't know. You need to figure out who can't know that you don't know and let them know that you know, *especially* if you don't know."

"That's ridiculous," I laughed. "There's no secret to success. You just have to be great at your job."

"No. That will get you nowhere. People will use your hard work to advance themselves and you'll be stuck in your cube forever."

"That's so cynical." Stevie was killing my buzz.

"One more thing – avoid CLMs like the plague."

"What's a CLM?" It sounded gross, like an STD.

"Career Limiting Move," Stevie replied. "Like sleeping with your boss. Bad news."

"Isn't that career-advancing?" I joked.

"We have a lot of work to do," Stevie shook his head. "We need to start at the beginning. I'm taking you shopping."

Needless to say, we did not address world peace that night. On the cab ride home and many martinis later, I questioned: (1) my ability to function at work tomorrow and (2) why can't straight men have gay conversational abilities, fashion sense or knowledge of good martini mixes? Stevie may not have had me at hello but he definitely had me at expensive and fabulous. Who knew?

My second date with Stevie was at Holt Renfrew over lunch hour the next day. Holt Renfrew had a feeling of luxurious authority and cold sterility similar to the Gisele offices but with more pretty and shiny things. I had never had the desire to set foot in Holt Renfrew before but it was fun with Stevie as my fashion coach.

Stevie flourished in his natural environment, like a deer released back into the wild. He moved swiftly and gracefully in his familiar surroundings, intensely focused, his senses heightened and gay-dar never sharper. As he scanned and assessed the merchandise, his muscles were tensed under his impeccably groomed garb, ready to pounce on the perfect accessory.

"So, what's the deal with Heidi and her entourage of BFFs?" I asked as we browsed the handbag section. It smelled like expensive leather and rich people. I imagine that this was like a pheromone to Stevie.

"Heidi's a sweetheart." Stevie said, carefully examining a handbag with more gold bling than my mother's jewelry box.

"Are we talking about the same Heidi?" I checked the price on a large brown bag emblazoned with initials. Strange, did they accidentally add another zero at the end of the price?

"She may come off as a little excessive," Stevie admitted, "but once you get to know her, she's as gentle as a smitten kitten."

"What in the world!? $1,700 for a purse? Who in their right mind —" I dropped the handbag like it was already burning my wallet.

"Shh!" Stevie looked around, embarrassed. "And be careful with Louis. Come, I'll show you the Coach handbags." I didn't care to ask about or apologize to Louis.

Stevie selected an elegant hobo bag from the shelf. "Ronnie," he said seriously, as if bestowing me with a great honour, "It's Coach time." He delicately placed the bag on my shoulder.

"It's nice," I assessed, admiring it in the mirror. Now I needed an expensive outfit worthy of the handbag. As advised by Stevie's mantra of *less is more*, I was dressed as minimally and simply as possible and all in black, as a temporary solution before Stevie could completely overhaul my wardrobe and destroy my credit rating.

With white gloves, I could pass as a mime, I observed. Or a Saturday Night Live Sprocket, if I slicked my hair back.

"It's wonderful," Stevie gushed. "Classic. And only a fraction of the price of the Louis Vuitton handbag you rejected. A Coach handbag is a good investment and keeps its value, like a Honda." Maybe I was bedazzled by the bright lights and all the pretty shiny things but it seemed like practical advice.

"So, how do I get on Chloe's good side?" I asked as I purchased the handbag at the cash. Or better yet, higher on The Tracker. I had a feeling that the two might be linked.

"You just need to stay away from her bad side." Stevie advised. "Her left side. Never take a photo from her left side and post it on Facebook." He flinched in memory of the incident. "And stay away from her territory. She's very protective. But other than that, lovely girl."

As the sales associate completed the sale and grandly handed me Holt Renfrew's pretty pink shopping bag, I felt special and girly. It was thrilling. I was overcome with strong feelings of freedom and guilt, like the morning after a one-night stand. Not that I had ever had one, but I imagine that's how it would feel.

Stevie stopped in his tracks and held his hand to his mouth, gasping. "Ronnie! OMG! Are you blushing from your Coach purchase? I'm so excited for you! You like good fashion!"

"You coached me to buy Coach!" I exclaimed. He hugged me and we jumped up and down together in joy. Apparently this was not an uncommon occurrence at Holt Renfrew because no one stopped to pay any heed.

"Honey, we can't stop now! Follow me!" Stevie clapped and led me upstairs.

"OK, so back to Chloe — forgive my ignorance but what is her territory?" Stevie was walking quickly, like a man on a mission, and I almost had to run to keep up.

"GiGi is launching a new line extension. She's been working on the launch since she joined the company. It's her baby and as per her Tracker, her ticket to promotion once it launches." Stevie was quickly rifling through a rack of expensive-looking dresses.

I tried to remember where Stevie's name was on Chloe's Tracker. He seemed so wise and omniscient, like a beauty marketing yogi. It was hard to believe he was still an entry-level marketer.

"What's the difference between Gisele and GiGi products?" I asked. After our Coach bonding experience, I was comfortable enough to ask stupid questions.

"Umm…nothing. Marketing. GiGi is targeted towards teens and twenty somethings — edgy, urban women who like to take risks."

I was baffled. "What? Gisele and GiGi are exactly the same product?"

"Not to an edgy urban risk-taking university student who wouldn't be caught dead buying Gisele products," Stevie corrected. "Just like you won't be caught dead wearing those harem pants again. By the way, MC Hammer called. He wants his pants back."

"Too late, I already burned them. Wow, I have a lot to learn," I was disenchanted by how manipulative Gisele's marketing seemed.

Stevie triumphantly held up a harlot-red wrap dress. "The Diane von Furstenberg wrap dress. Nothing short of brilliance. Be still my heart."

"Be still my credit card." I protested. "It's not my style."

"Ronnie, you have a great bod and you need to show it off. Gisele is throwing a party to celebrate gaining the #1 share position in the Lip market. You are going to make your grand entrance in this dress. You vixen." He handed over the dress with authority. "And you need to fix your hair and get decent shoes, but we'll deal with that later," he added.

Needless to say, we didn't quite get to cover world peace on our second date either. I returned to Gisele's offices with an empty stomach and a full credit card statement.

Chapter 4: Forbidden Fruit

"Welcome to Gisele!" Savannah was back from New York and appeared at my cube like a pimple before a first date: without warning or welcome. Luckily, her expensive fragrance preceded her so I was not as startled by her aggressively sudden appearance as I was by her imposing presence.

Under the harsh lights of Gisele's sterile environment, Savannah no longer had the friendly, cool-boss guise that she embodied during our coffee chat. She now had an air of self-entitled superiority and power that you dare not question. I found myself slightly cowering in her shadow. She had long curly hair, which she styled like a lion's mane. Or Medusa.

She ceremoniously leaned in to kiss me. Unaccustomed to this greeting, I panicked, not knowing which way to lean, and we ended up kissing on the lips. I flushed as Savannah burst out in what sounded like mocking laughter, throwing back her lion's mane. Mateo would have enjoyed this moment.

"Sorry," I mumbled.

"Follow me," Savannah announced and took off. I ran to keep up with her as she strode purposely to her office.

Savannah was seated importantly at her desk when I entered, breathless. How can that lady walk so fast with four-inch platform heels? Did she disapparate like a Harry Potter witch?

Savannah's office had the same minimalistic coldness as the front lobby. Behind her desk was a huge, framed poster of a stark naked model, strategically positioned to hide her nudity, standing by a frozen tree in a fantastical garden. Lipstick tubes hung from the tree instead of apples. The colours were frosted shades of blue and white except for the lipstick tubes and the model's lips, which were slut-red. The distressed model held a lipstick to her open mouth.

"It's the Forbidden Fruit campaign that I launched last year." Savannah said, following my stare. "It's the most successful launch we've ever had in Canada. As a result, we received the #1 share position in Lip for the first time ever."

"It's amazing," I said truthfully. Whether I thought it was amazingly stupid or amazingly ridiculous was a detail that was not necessary to share.

Savannah smiled proudly and patted her lion mane. She looked like a scary clown, except with nicer make-up. "So. Welcome to the real MBA. How have you been enjoying your first two weeks?"

"It's been great!" I said, putting Stevie's Cardinal Rule #2 into effect. "The people have been really nice and Heidi has been so helpful. I'm totally up to speed now on the Lip and Nail segment."

"Great. What do you think of our Forbidden Fruit lipstick?" It was posed more as a test question than a question of curiosity.

"Oh, I don't wear makeup," I blurted, brilliantly failing the test.

There was a chilling silence as Savannah frowned, confused. "That's impossible."

I sat agonizingly still, almost afraid to breathe, frozen in silent fear.

"Did Heidi give you access to the product closet? You must immerse yourself in the product. How can you market Gisele if you don't know our product and how it compares to the competition?"

"You're right," I replied, exhaling with relief and making a mental note for Stevie to take me to all the competitive makeup counters. "Heidi encouraged me to immerse myself in the business plans and the research first."

Savannah raised an eyebrow. "I will speak with Heidi." I flinched.

Shit, I did not mean to get Heidi in trouble.

"I am sure you are wondering what your first assignment is," she leaned forward onto her sparse mahogany desk. I nodded obediently and emphatically. "Have you heard about G-Spot?"

I wasn't sure how to answer but I'm sure my face betrayed my discomfort and confusion.

"GiGi's Gi-Spot launch," she clarified, barely hiding her irritation. "It's our biggest launch this year. A team has been working on it for a year. It's GiGi's follow-up to the Forbidden Fruit campaign."

I displayed what I believed to be appropriate expressions of awe and excitement.

"You have a meeting with the Vice President of Human Resources."

Terror struck my heart. What? Have I failed Oompa Loompa already? Maybe someone from Human Resources overheard my rant at the Betty Ford Clinic.

"Etienne's office is located on the executive floor. Your meeting with Etienne is scheduled right now." This was my signal to leave immediately. I was relieved to be released from her clutches.

I took the mirrored elevators to the thirty-seventh floor, looking back at my deer-in-headlight expression. The elevators opened opposite a flat screen TV, playing Gisele's advertising so that visitors were instantly greeted with an onslaught of branding.

I watched the TV spot currently playing on the screen. A supermodel was alone on the roof of a downtown high rise, as supermodels are apt to do, with gusts of hurricane-like wind whipping her long hair and dress around her. Helicopters circled around her, filled with shouting paparazzi, snapping photographs as the model reveled in her freakishly unnatural beauty.

"Don't hate me because I'm beautiful," the model pouted. "Love me." I instantly hated her. The TV spot ended in a burst of blinding flash photography and the words *Love Me* beside a bottle of fragrance.

I waited with trepidation in the unwelcoming executive lobby, avoiding the glare of the equally unwelcoming receptionist. Oompa Loompa soon emerged, greeting me like a long lost relative, enveloped in strong cologne. It did not make me love him but reminded me about our dream in a bottle conversation. I had gone through my dry run with Savannah and fortunately was able to avoid kissing Oompa Loompa on the lips.

He and his cologne beckoned me into his office. He appropriately offered me chocolate.

"Has Savannah told you about the purpose of this meeting?" He asked after I feebly turned down the chocolate.

"No," I croaked.

"Don't worry," he assured me. "It is good news for you. Please. Have a seat."

I sunk, relieved, into the leather armchair. There was no reason for Savannah to send me terrified to the executive offices other than to exercise her power to inflict fear.

"Gi-Spot, as you know, is our most high profile launch this year. I want you to start your career associated with the success of this launch." It was even more uncomfortable for me to hear Oompa Loompa speak about Gi-Spot. The only thing that interested me about this launch was why they chose such an absurd name for it.

"That is very kind of you but isn't Chloe managing the launch?" I remembered Stevie's advice regarding Chloe's territory.

"My dear, it takes more than one person to plan and execute a successful launch. The team has been doing a great job but they can't do it all. I am pleased to give you a very special assignment. It is the Gi-Spot launch party!"

Seriously? I completed my MBA to plan a party for some sort of sexual makeup?

"It sounds great," I lied, praying that the launch wasn't GiGi's foray into sex toys. I'm quite sure this would not be recognized by Amnesty International as transferable experience.

However, as I had previously experienced, Oompa Loompa knew how to close the deal. "There will be Gisele executives from the New York office at this party. It will be great exposure for you. If you are successful at this party, it can very well lead to a transfer to the New York office." And with that, I accepted the Forbidden Fruit.

I was seated in the cafeteria at lunchtime later that day, waiting for Stevie to join me when Chloe confronted me. "Is it true? Are you planning the Gi-Spot party?" I was caught off guard and unprepared. How did she find out so quickly? I looked around furtively for Stevie.

"I've been working on my Gi-Spot all year!" Chloe exclaimed loudly. People seated close by stopped talking to observe the unusual confrontation.

"The launch is still yours," I said, trying to clam her down. "I'm just planning the party. That's all."

"You can't take my Gi-Spot party!" She exclaimed and stormed off. I tried not to laugh at how this statement may be misconstrued. I hoped that those around us knew about the Gi-Spot launch.

"Gi-Spot is a product launch," I explained to the people at the table beside me. They looked blankly back at me. "We're not talking about the actual, you know, *sexual* G spot." I further clarified. "I'm not planning a sex party or anything."

Disinterested, they resumed their conversation. Am I the only one uncomfortable with this name?

"I heard! The Gi-Spot party!" Stevie rushed to join me. "That's fabulous!"

"I'm encroaching on Chloe's territory," I sighed, "She hates me."

"Well, of course. You'll only be working for a few months on the party, while Chloe's been slaving for a full year, and you're both going to share in the glory. Well done, you vixen! My, my, you are Etienne's little pet, aren't you?"

"Well, he did say it was my ticket to New York," I agreed. "Now I just have to figure out what Gi-Spot is."

"Don't you all?" Stevie winked.

LATER THAT NIGHT Gisele threw their 'We're #1!' celebration, a private party at the Panorama Lounge and Restaurant on the fifty-first floor of the Manulife Centre, which had easily the best view in Toronto. Gisele had strategically chosen a venue that made us feel on top of the world. It was a lavish proclamation of Gisele's Lip leadership.

The night began with the President of Gisele Canada giving a victory speech, which could have easily been borrowed from any political leader after winning a world war. Our President, Klaus Veicht, was from Germany and his accent seemed eerily fitting as he declared Gisele's world domination and swiftness in conquering the Canadian lip market. Drunk with power and expensive wine, we clapped and cheered in solidarity, his cosmetic army.

It seemed that Klaus was born for world domination. Veicht was German for fight. Klaus was transferred to Canada after his success leading several Western European markets to market leadership. He was still quite young and was destined to continue the momentum in larger markets. I wondered if, as a child, Klaus exhibited any early signs that he would take over the world with makeup, like playing with his mother's makeup rather than G.I. Joe. Maybe he played with makeup and G.I. Joe at the same time.

Stevie had me dolled up in my new Diane von Furstenberg dress. He had also taken me to MAC after work to apply my makeup, as per Savannah's advice. I had never put this much care and attention into my appearance but it was admittedly exhilarating. As I stood with Stevie by the bar sipping a glass of Pinot Grigio, I felt like a veritable vixen. Across the bar, Chloe's jealousy was burning through her retinas as she shot me cut-eye. Heidi did a double take, as if she did not recognize me in fashionable clothes. Jasmine Tit stood up straighter, if that was possible. I smiled, as vixens do.

"So, how is Savannah?" Stevie questioned. I was avoiding her, lest she kill my vixen mojo. I saw her talking and laughing with colleagues, champagne flute in hand, and looking phony.

"I think she gets angry when she's sober," I answered. "And what's with the hair?"

"I think her hair is very fashion forward. It becomes her," Stevie disagreed.

Oompa Loompa approached Stevie and me. "Veronica, you look lovely tonight! As do you, Stevie."

"Hi, Etienne. What a fantastic night! We were just discussing Veronica's wonderful new assignment," Stevie lied, smooth like butter.

"Of course, of course, wonderful news. Stevie, may I borrow your girlfriend for a moment?" Oompa Loompa led me across the room. "Come, I would like you to meet Caden, the Vice President of GiGi. In addition to your duties on Savannah's portfolio, you will also temporarily report into Caden for the Gi-Spot party."

We stopped in front of a startlingly handsome man and, never having been in the presence of the most beautiful man in the world, I was instantly a hot mess.

"Caden, this is Veronica," Oompa Loompa introduced us, which was fortunate because I had temporarily forgotten my name. "She will be managing the Gi-Spot launch party." Caden shook my hand and I think I may have whimpered.

"Great to have you on the team, Veronica." Caden smiled and I swooned, no longer a vixen, but a fair maiden.

"Great…you," I managed to croak in a feeble attempt to prove to Caden that I was not mute. My mouth was dehydrated and my vixen mojo had evaporated. I suddenly realized that my hands were quite large and flabby. I panicked, not knowing where to hide them. I excused myself before I lost control of my bodily functions and somehow made it back to Stevie. He was talking to Mateo who was sporting a black shirt unnecessarily unbuttoned to display his sparse chest hair.

"I think I need a shot of Jägermeister," I said to Stevie, still bewildered from the encounter.

"Oh, you must have met Caden," Stevie guessed correctly. "I'll be right back." And he unwisely left me unattended with Mateo.

"Veronica, you look hot!" Mateo salivated.

"Are my hands large and flabby?" I asked, deeply concerned of my recent discovery.

"No babe, you're perfectly proportioned, like a Barbie doll." He grabbed my hand and twirled me around.

I snapped out of my stupor upon Mateo's grimy touch. I looked around for Purell and saw Caden looking at me from across the room with amusement. My heart started beating irregularly and my breathing became laboured. *He's laughing at my hands!* I had the strong urge to run towards him in slow motion and make him love my hands. But instead I ran towards Stevie who was returning with water.

"Don't leave me alone with Mateo!" I hissed as I clutched weakly at Stevie's arm with my man-hands.

"Who? Matthew? He's harmless." I was beginning to think that Stevie was a very bad judge of character.

"Stevie, please be honest with me. Are my hands abnormally large?" I asked, desperate.

"What? No, you're hands are perfectly normal. What's wrong with you? You're all flushed and hysterical. Are you coming down with a fever? Here, drink some water." He replaced my wine glass, miraculously still in hand, with a bottle of water.

I hastily drank half the bottle in one swig. "Whoa, I was thirsty."

"Ronnie, you're cut off. Do you want me to call you a cab?"

"Is Caden single?" I whispered.

"Caden is your boss," Stevie grabbed my shoulders and looked me in the eyes. "You need to pull it together."

"You're right, you're right." I assented, nodding vigourously. "Am I out of my mind? Crazy! Cuckoo!"

"Yes, you are." Stevie agreed and carefully took my arm to lead me to the coat room.

I disobediently scanned the room for Caden and saw Chloe laughing in an exaggerated manner with him. I was overcome with unnaturally strong feelings of possession and jealousy. My eyes narrowed. How can she conduct herself in his presence in such a normal manner? Now confident in the normality of my hands, I vowed that I would be exceedingly normal around Caden, putting Chloe's normal to shame.

And with that, the Gi-Spot launch party became even more important to my advancement. Not only was this going to facilitate my transfer to New York but it would also put me in Caden's good graces. After all, he was only going to be my boss until I threw the most awesome party in the world.

Chapter 5: Nightmare

THAT NIGHT I HAD A nightmare. I am lost, walking aimlessly through Gisele's sterile cubicle maze, looking for my cubicle. Everyone is staring at me in horror and disgust. I'm wearing my MC Hammer harem pants and my face is covered with red lego-like acne. "Don't hate me because I'm ugly," I plead. "Love me." Stevie appears and tries to spritz me with a dream in a bottle but it smells like cow poo. He cannot stand the smell of ugly and slinks away in defeat. "Come back, gay boyfriend," I cry out but he is gone. "My boyfriend isn't gay," Jasmine Tit declares as she appears before me and then instantly disappears.

I enter a boardroom covered in mirrors. The mirrors are distorted, like a crazy house of mirrors at a circus or a bikini change room. Klaus is sitting at the end of a long table that looks like a runway, with Caden and Oompa Loompa on either side of him. Klaus is dressed in military gear. Oompa Loompa is in a jester outfit and is looking at me through a monocle. Caden is dressed like a cowboy from the Wild West. They have long handlebar mustaches that they are twirling with their fingers. They are laughing, the kind of evil madman laughter that one makes when one takes over the world with makeup.

I see my acne-covered face, contorted and reflected, in a million mirrors and I scream in agony. "Noooooooo! I'm uuuuglyyyyyyy!"

"Get out of here," they are yelling at me. "You're so ugly you'll break the mirrors." I turn to run but I can't find the doors. The mirrors start to break and cave in on us. "Off with her head, off with her head!" Klaus yells.

I woke up sweating. I looked in the mirror and breathed a sigh of relief. Not a blemish on my face.

After memorizing encyclopedic volumes of information on Gisele's Lip & Nail segment for the last few weeks, Savannah decided that I'd be better placed with Sydney in Gisele Eye as there are more new product launches to plan in Eye than Lip & Nail. Plus, Gisele Lip & Nail were still selling like crazy, riding the wave of the Forbidden Fruit campaign.

I joined Sydney in preparing for the dreaded Marketing Review which was to take place in a mere seven days. Savannah thought it would be a great learning experience for me to present. The Marketing Review was the proverbial throwing of the sacrificial virgins into the fire, or the chance for the junior marketers to cut their teeth presenting to Gisele executives.

"What kind of questions do they ask you?" I asked Sydney, started to get worried.

"Anything." Sydney answered. "Just don't say that you don't know. That's like saying 'please fire me'."

"But how do you remember everything?"

Sydney handed me a huge binder with about fifty tab dividers. "The Eye Bible. Don't dare enter a boardroom without it. We update it every month. Your turn."

Unlike Heidi, Sydney was generous with sharing, or giving me, work. I didn't know how I would possibly find time to get up to speed on the Gisele Eye business, update the Eye Bible and help Sydney with the presentation because I was also invited to any meeting to do with Gisele Eye. Since I was new, I participated in countless meetings as if I were a fly on the wall. From this vantage point, these meetings seemed to really get in the way of getting things done. People would spin like whirling dervishes over every detail until dizzy with deliberation.

My days were caught up in the whirl of these meetings and I found myself only starting to get any work done at 5 pm, just when Sydney was leaving. Sydney was happy to completely offload the presentation on me. I could see now why Heidi was bitter.

The Marketing Review presentation had a template that we updated manually every couple of months. This template was designed by a sadist to be a painstakingly laborious and time-consuming exercise of analysis paralysis. The rest of the presentation was a dog and pony show. To that end, we clogged up our computer servers trying to make the presentations look pretty with lots of images and embedded videos.

The other particularly unpleasant part of the presentation prep was Savannah's reviews. She seemed to derive pleasure in ripping apart the fruits of my labour, her scribbled revisions cutting through the page like insults. The last round of review by Savannah was meticulous word-smithing and layout editing, another curious method of wasting time and energy.

Although I had worked almost every waking hour to learn the business and prepare a monumental presentation in less than two weeks, I was a nervous mess on the day of the presentation. As per Stevie's counsel, my hair was pulled back into a low and loose chignon. I was dressed in a simple black dress and short-sleeved cream blazer from Banana Republic that I purchased with Stevie's approval after convincing him, in protection of my credit card balance, that I did not want to invest in a Gucci suit, even if it was the Mercedes Benz of business suits. He consented even though he thought that my purchase was safe and boring, like a Volvo.

I cancelled all my morning meetings to review the presentation but was unable to concentrate due to an exceptionally nervous bladder. When I passed by Sydney's desk on my seventh trip the bathroom, she stopped me.

"Where are you going?" she demanded.

"Um…to the bathroom. Is that OK?"

"What? Are you crazy? You can't leave your desk! You are the holder of the Eye Bible. If Savannah calls for information and you're not at your desk, you are in deep shit."

"I can't pee? What am I supposed to do? Wear a diaper?"

"No, you just don't drink." Sydney answered, as if dehydrating myself was the most obvious option in the world.

"What are the chances that Savannah will call me the one minute that I go to the bathroom?"

"I would run if I were you," Sydney advised. I paused to consider the warning then ran like the wind to the bathroom. My phone was ringing when I returned, speed walking, to my cubicle. *You're kidding.* Panicked, I grabbed for the phone.

"It's Sydney. Savannah called. They're running an hour late so they're going to work through lunch to stay on track. We're on at noon. Remember, we need to go fifteen minutes early to dress the room."

"Do you know if Savannah tried calling me?"

"Sorry, I don't know."

"Great." I was now in deep shit for not peeing my pants.

At quarter to noon, I arrived punctually at Sydney's cubicle with a cart full of items to dress the room but she was not there. She wasn't waiting for me in the boardroom either. There were two boardrooms at Gisele. The presentations alternated between these two boardrooms to allow the following team to dress the room. Dressing the room was a two-person fifteen-minute minute ordeal. You had to arrange your products meticulously like shrines to the makeup gods throughout the room. You also had to overkill the room with branding – posters and banners of your portfolio's most recent advertising around the perimeter of the room. The desired effect was as if the room vomited your brand.

Since Sydney was AWOL, I embarked on the task solo. At around five minutes to noon, as I stood admiring my work, Sydney ran into the room, uncharacteristically frantic.

"Change of room, change of room! We're in the Mascara Boardroom! Didn't you get my email?" I had turned off my email alert so that I didn't get distracted. Note to self: there are three boardrooms at Gisele.

Sydney started grabbing products and wildly throwing them into the cart.

"Grab the posters and run!" She bolted out of the room with the cart.

"Wait! Where's the Mascara boardroom?" I gathered the posters and banners and ran in the same direction as Sydney. The posters were large and cumbersome and made running down the long hall quite challenging.

"Where's the Mascara boardroom?" I yelled blindly, the posters blocking my eyesight, to the first person I ran into. Unfortunately, it was Caden. Of course, I run into the man of my dreams just when I looked like I escaped from an insane asylum, sweating, panting, and hair astray. I was probably foaming at the mouth.

He laughed. "Let me guess? Marketing Review? The room's just down the hall, to your right. Do you need help?"

"No, I'm fine!" I continued clamoring ungracefully down the hall. Apparently a combination of humiliation and fear-induced adrenaline gave me the ability to utter a coherent sentence in Caden's presence. In any case, whatever it was, I'm sure it was extremely unattractive.

I arrived in the Mascara Boardroom, breathless and shaking. I dropped the posters in a heap on the ground.

"Take a deep breath! Calm down, just calm down!" Sydney yelled, frenzied. She grabbed the posters. Two of them were visibly damaged during my mad dash down the hall. "Shit, we can't use these. Stay here. I'll get some back-up posters. Hurry, hurry, fix the products!"

The products were disrespectfully piled on the boardroom table. The makeup gods would be insulted. I rushed maniacally around the room, throwing products around haphazardly. Sydney ran back in the room in a couple of minutes empty-handed, unable to find back-up posters. We decided unwisely to place the visibly damaged posters in the furthest corners of the room. The room looked like it was dressed by drunken sailors.

Savannah, Medusa snakes well-behaved, and the designer-suited executives started filing seriously into the room. The designer suits looked like they were angry at the oxygen in the room. Sydney motioned to me to fix my hair. As the designer suits took their seats, I tried to squeeze my loose hair back into my once sophisticated chignon. Sydney shook her head. I removed the chignon. She widened her eyes and shook her head vigorously. As I put my hair into a sloppy ponytail, I realized that I forgot the Eye Bible in the other boardroom. I mouthed the word "bible" to Sydney but she didn't understand. Resorting to charades, I put my hands together in prayer position and looked up at the heavens. At this point, I noticed the designer suits and Savannah now seated and staring at me, unimpressed. I suddenly had the urge to pee again.

"Hi, I'm Veronica." I greeted them awkwardly with a wave. I only recognized Klaus and Savannah but none of the designer suits bothered to return my introduction. I cleared my throat and moved to the laptop. Sydney had the presentation ready to go. However, it wasn't going. I clicked the mouse and banged the keyboard increasingly frantically and violently.

"Just a minute," I filled the tense air with nervous laughter. The silence from their end was palpable.

My audience was not amused. Sydney came to the front of the room with a USB key, inserted it into the laptop and opened the presentation for me. It was not what one would describe as a smooth start. Maybe I should have prayed to the IT gods instead of the makeup gods before the presentation.

I stumbled through the presentation, struggling to read the slides as if I needed glasses. Klaus interrupted me halfway through the presentation. "Why are there so many fucking slides?"

I stood open-mouthed and mute, staring back at him.

"It is so fucking long. Get to the point."

"Um..." I looked at Savannah and Sydney for help. They avoided my eyes. All the extra slides were added as per Savannah's request. "Well... uh... we wanted to make sure that we were prepared for —"

"Bull shit," he responded. You could say that the presentation wasn't going so well.

He leaned back in the chair and crossed his arms. "What percentage of Gisele consumers buy multiple Gisele mascara products simultaneously? For example: volumizing mascara and lengthening mascara."

I did not think that he was open to debating whether volumizing and lengthening mascara were the same thing. My mind was blank. All I could think of to say was, '*please don't fire me*'.

"About seventy percent," Sydney piped up. I frowned. That didn't seem right.

"Good. We need to get that number up to 100%. No one should be happy with just one mascara brush," he scoffed at the ridiculousness of the notion. "We have to make women want – no – *need* to buy all of our mascara products. I want to see your plan to accomplish this at the next Marketing Review. Is that clear?" I nodded like his puppet, accepting the absurd challenge. The designer suits stood up and filed out of the room, leaving Sydney and me alone to clean up the mess.

"Great meeting!" Sydney looked ready to high-five me.

"Do you mean the one that just happened? Are you kidding me? It was a total shit show." If I had made any progress on Chloe's Tracker, this would have set me back.

"Don't worry, you'll learn to think on your feet."

"You mean lie on your feet? There's no way seventy percent of our consumers buy different Gisele mascara products at the same time!"

Sydney shrugged. "Close enough. I rounded up. You'll learn. Can you take care of this?" she gestured around the room. "I have a meeting to run to. Thanks!"

Sure enough, in a debrief with Savannah, she used Sydney's quick thinking as an example of how to conduct oneself professionally in a meeting. Savannah's Medusa hair had awakened as a teeming mass of hissing snakes.

"And whatever religious rituals you perform before a presentation, I don't care, but please keep them to yourself." As Savannah continued to explain all the ways in which I was incompetent, I found myself profusely apologizing for not being able to control my biological functions, my apparent praying and my bad hair. Her Medusa snakes sneered and stuck their tongues out at me.

Once I was satisfactorily humbled, Savannah moved on to what I suppose was the cheerleader part of the debrief. "Klaus's challenge is incredibly inspirational. I think we're going to do great things under his leadership. Let's make his challenge your new obsession. And keep the next presentation short and sweet. Klaus doesn't like long presentations."

No shit, Sherlock. This would have been a helpful revelation before I slaved over the "fucking long" presentation for the past two weeks. I felt like curling up in the corner of my cube with a bottle of Jäger crying over my lost competency.

After my debrief with Savannah, I had a much more supportive session with Stevie. I described every agonizing detail of the Marketing Review, leaving out my unfortunate encounter with Caden. Stevie grimaced and covered his eyes for most of it as if it were a horror movie.

"Do I not have the right to pee?" I asked. "Isn't depriving us of our right to pee akin to slave labour?"

"Well, no but I guess you just have to pee strategically...listen drama queen, you forgot all about Cardinal Rule #2," Stevie proclaimed. "If you don't know, you need to lie with confidence. Sydney is the best at it because most of the time she doesn't know."

"You're right. I don't know why I doubted your rules." I rubbed my eyes. "I worked so hard and it was all for nothing. In the end, I looked like a complete loser. Sydney did nothing, lied and was the hero of the day."

"Well, I wouldn't beat yourself too much over it, but this *is* a beauty company. Appearance matters. Now Savannah may take a little bit of a tough love approach —"

"Yeah, except without the love," I corrected.

"Yes, but she's a brilliant marketer – one of the best at Gisele. Think of it this way – you have the best of both worlds – learning from one the best marketers and one of the best bullshitters at Gisele. Who can ask for more? You are one lucky gal!"

My performance at the Marketing Review had undoubtedly set me back a few paces on my path to New York but Stevie renewed my faith in the process. Not quite feeling like a lucky gal, I was now open to learning the rules of the game. I opened a new document on my computer and recorded Stevie's Cardinal Rules. I paused to reflect upon my most recent learning and added *'4. Pee Strategically'.*

Chapter 6: Congratulations

I hadn't seen Jackie, Lindsay and Calista since my one-week anniversary celebration at the Betty Ford Clinic over a month ago. We had plans to meet after work at Hemingway's, a local pub just two blocks from where I worked in Yorkville. I was excited to see them and catch up. This was the longest span of time I had gone without seeing them.

"Well hello, Miss Yorkville," Jackie greeted me as I ran in late from work, garbed in yet another Volvo outfit.

"Hi! I miss you guys! It's been so long!" There was a flurry of hugging.

"You look so professional, I almost didn't recognize you!" I think that was a compliment from Lindsay.

"Yeah, you actually combed your hair and —" Jackie stopped as she noticed I was wearing makeup. "Oh my God, are you wearing makeup?"

"Well, it *is* my job. Speaking of which, here's your makeup, Madame, as requested." I had selected several bestsellers from the Forbidden Fruit collection for Jackie. "I'm so sorry I've been AWOL these past few weeks. Work has swallowed me whole but my hours should get better now that I'm up to speed."

"It better!" Jackie warned.

"What's been going on in your lives? I'm dying to know, and I'm dying of thirst." I waved down a server to order a drink.

Calista, Lindsay and Jackie then inundated me with accusations of screening their calls and never getting back to them.

"Are you guys telling me off?" I laughed. "I'm sorry! I promise my hours are going to get better because I simply refuse to continue working this much." The server appeared and I requested a Pinot Grigio.

Lindsay gasped. "What? What happened to your regular gin & tonic?"

"Wine's better for your heart." I shrugged.

"Yeah, health is my top criteria in selecting an alcoholic beverage. Cheers," Jackie winked, taking a sip of her dirty martini.

"I don't know if it's the clothes or makeup but you look different," Lindsay observed me closely. "Not that it's a bad thing…" she added, reassuringly.

"No," Calista said. "It's just been so long that we forget what you look like."

"Please," I rolled my eyes.

"OK ladies," Jackie announced, "You've said it before, but now it's confirmed. I've officially dated every guy in Toronto."

"I knew I was right," Calista shook her head, already laughing, and we braced ourselves for another hilarious Jackie dating story.

"So I'm on this date and the guy looks familiar so I ask him whether we've met before but he doesn't recognize me. Halfway through our date, I'm super annoyed by the way he holds his spoon. Like this —" Jackie demonstrated what appeared to be normal spoon-holding etiquette. We nodded understandingly even though we didn't understand, "So annoying. And then I realize I went on a date with him four years ago."

We laughed, not in the least surprised. "I've literally dated every single guy in Toronto and now I'm starting all over again!"

"Maybe the timing is right four years later. How did the date go?" Lindsay asked, ever the helpless romantic.

"Just as bad as it did four years ago." Jackie replied. "The spoon."

"Maybe you need to expand to the 'burbs," I suggested.

"No," Jackie shuddered, "I can't do it."

"OK, so Jackie has officially dated every single guy in Toronto and —" Calista started to say.

"I think some of them may have been married," Jackie corrected. "In retrospect," she added quickly, seeing our shocked expressions.

"I officially completed my PhD!" Calista finished her sentence, effectively distracting us from the awkward moment.

"No way! Congratulations! You're officially a rocket scientist. Or economist, same thing. This deserves a massive celebration!" I hugged Calista.

"Or a massive vacation," Calista laughed.

"We're going all out and throwing a huge party for her," Lindsay said, smiling at Calista.

"What about my congratulations? Dating all of Toronto is just as hard as getting a PhD." Jackie joked.

"No doubt. That takes a special skill. If there were a PhD in dating, you would have already earned it. I could put in a request with Harvard." Calista offered.

"Oh, shut up, you genius. Not to take away from Calista's accomplishment, *obviously* more important than dating all of Toronto, but I can't believe you haven't noticed yet." Jackie turned to me expectantly.

"Noticed what?" I was confused.

"I'm engaged!" Lindsay exclaimed, throwing her left hand up to my face to show me her shiny engagement ring.

"That's amazing! Congratulations!" I was excited for Lindsay but felt an incredible pang of guilt that I hadn't noticed her very noticeable ring. "When did he propose? Tell me all about it." I insisted. This was bound to happen sooner or later. Justin was Lindsay's university sweetheart and they were perfect for one another.

"Last week, it was our five-year anniversary." As Lindsay described the incredibly romantic proposal, I realized that Jackie and Calista hadn't chimed in to the congratulations and weren't reacting to the story the same way I was. It didn't take a rocket scientist to figure out that they already knew. Come to think of it, Calista's announcement did not seem like new news to Jackie and Lindsay, either.

"I'm sorry Lindsay, did you try to call me and tell me?" I was mortified at my self-involvement. Completing a PhD and getting engaged were some of the most important events in my friends' lives and I missed it because I was working on a 'fucking long' presentation.

"I'm sorry, I wanted to tell you all at once but I couldn't hold it in..."

"No, no don't apologize, it was my fault. Congratulations. Your ring is beautiful."

"But I did manage to keep one secret." Lindsay smiled coyly and paused, to build up the suspense.

"Spit it out, you're killing me!" Jackie exclaimed.

"I want the three of you to be my bridesmaids!" That ensued another round of cheers and hugging and maybe a few tears.

Once we settled down, Jackie turned the attention to me. "So I've dated all of Toronto, Calista got her PhD and Lindsay got engaged. What have you done with yourself in the past month, missy?"

"Well when you put it that way, I've been an incredible failure."

"Boo hoo. You better give us a better answer as to why you've been hiding yourself for the past month." Jackie demanded.

"I have a gay boyfriend."

There was a moment of silence. "Why are you dating him if he's gay?" Lindsay finally asked. Calista looked equally confused.

"No, no, he's not really my boyfriend, more like a platonic boyfriend, but gay."

"I don't get it." Calista still looked confused. Apparently rocket scientists don't understand everything.

This was more Jackie's territory. She jumped in with an alarmingly accurate summary. "He's Team Veronica; tells her she's gorgeous; he's super fun and hilarious; makes her laugh; loves fashion and shopping. He says things like 'you look fa-bu today' and 'oh no you dih-int!' and 'hollah at ya girl!'"

"That's not true. He has much better pronunciation than that." I didn't realize until Jackie summarized it so bluntly that Stevie was essentially President of the Veronica Fan Club, present member count: 1.

"So if you got a heterosexual boyfriend, would you be cheating on him?" Lindsay asked me.

"No, no, it's just a silly expression that I thought was funny." I gave up. "And clearly no one else does."

"I just don't get it," Calista repeated.

"Anyway, you guys would love him. I can't wait for you to meet him."

"Is he responsible for your new look?" Lindsay asked.

"It's not a new look, I'm just wearing new clothes. But yes, he helped me shop for them."

"And neither of you have any romantic feelings for one another?" Calista was still trying to crack the gay boyfriend code.

"No! Forget gay boyfriend. He's my friend. And he's been helping me fit in and get up to speed at work, kind of like a mentor. He's the only person who's nice to me at Gisele. I probably would have been fired by now without his help."

"What are his motives for helping you? Are you sure he's gay?" Lindsay asked.

"He's definitely gay. Wow, you guys are really territorial. Don't worry, it's not him that's keeping me away from you guys. It's my job." I hadn't expected my friends to be so distrusting of my new gay boyfriend. I was going to have to figure out how to get Stevie into the circle of trust.

"How's the job been going?" Calista asked.

"Um…it's less horrible. But I just got a great assignment. I'm organizing a launch party for an important product launch."

"What product launch? Can you tell us?" Lindsay asked.

"I can on two conditions. One that you keep it confidential and second that you don't laugh."

They wholeheartedly agreed but when I told them about Gi-Spot they howled with laughter.

"You realize that we're going to make fun of you for the rest of your life," Jackie said after the laughter died down.

"You've just gone from saving the world to throwing a sex party!" Lindsay pointed out. "What happened to Veronica?"

"I guess no one's going to congratulate me?" I asked in jest, to cover up my disappointment at my friends' lack of excitement for my achievement.

"Why don't you incorporate a charity element into the party?" Calista suggested, in her usual genius way. "That way you can do both – save the world and throw a sex party."

"That's a great idea, Calista. Thank you. Now maybe you can help me with my other problem." Jackie leaned in, all ears. "For this party, I report into the most beautiful man in the world. He's a VP and I have a huge crush on him. It's a little bit of a problem."

"Congratulations!" Jackie exclaimed.

"Do you think if I throw the best party in the world he'll fall in love with me?" I joked.

"Absolutely," Jackie assured.

"I didn't think corporate was your type." Lindsay remarked.

I didn't think I had a type. "Since when was hot not my type? What do you think my type is?"

"I don't know…like, hot carpenter." Lindsay answered. Jackie nodded approvingly.

"Yeah, maybe…if my life were a porn movie."

"Be careful." Calista warned. "This has bad news written all over it."

"I just need to be careful until I throw the party and he's no longer my boss. Right, Jackie?"

Jackie nodded in support. "I want to see him. I wonder if I've ever dated him?"

"No, it's not OK. He's a VP and you're an entry level marketer." Calista pointed out.

Lindsay nodded in agreement. "Jackie, you're outnumbered. It's definitely *not* OK to become romantically involved with your VP – especially if he's married. Please tell me he's not married."

"That is a very good point. I don't know." I had some sleuthing to do… "Anyway, I need to get back to the office."

"What?" Lindsay looked at her watch. "It's past nine o'clock. That's disgusting."

"I need to get started on this sex party planning thing. I've been neglecting it because I was working on a fucking long presentation."

"Your workplace sounds like so much fun." Jackie said. "Or…are you trying to catch a glimpse of VP Hottie tonight?"

"No, I'm trying to impress VP Hottie with my party planning skills." I got up and put my jacket on.

"Well, here's to saving the world." Lindsay said as I bid farewell and Jackie requested more makeup. I hurried back to the office, a little bit of concern over my friends' distrust gnawing at my insides.

Chapter 7: Existential Crisis

ONE OF THE FIRST THINGS that Klaus did when he arrived at Gisele Canada, in disgust of Canadian coffee, was set up a premium European coffee shop in Gisele's atrium, complete with a full-time barista and German-named coffee drinks. This put him in good standing with the masses, at least until they met him. European coffee was certainly not my first priority in terms of work benefits, but it was admittedly a generous perk. I was not a coffee fan myself but occasionally allowed Stevie to drag me along as he enjoyed his daily *Verkehrt* (latte macchiato). On our latest coffee run I encountered Caden who was drinking an espresso, somehow managing to make that little cup look super sexy and manly.

"Veronica! What are you drinking?" He waved the barista over and smiled at me. His teeth were dazzling. I was mesmerized by his dimples. "What's your pleasure?"

"You." I said without thinking. Caden raised his eyebrows. Stevie kicked me and I jolted back to my senses. "I mean you – your – what you're drinking…is what I meant…by you." Stevie laughed loudly to cover up the awkward moment and I joined in weakly.

"Ah, espresso, that will get you going in the morning." Caden smiled magnificently again, unaffected by my school girl adoration. I kicked the espresso back, like it was a shot.

"Whoa! It's meant to be savoured but…whatever works for you," Caden laughed and the heavens opened up in appreciation of the beautiful sound of his laughter.

"Wow, that – that works." I felt my heart beating maniacally, not knowing whether it was caused by sudden and excessive caffeine intake or Caden's proximity. "That's strong shi – stuff. I like it!"

"Good. How's the party planning going?"

"Great!" I lied. The truth is, I hadn't been able to connect with Chloe for a transition meeting. I had tried setting up several meetings over the last week but she kept blowing me off.

"How about we meet and catch up over an espresso?" *OMG, is he asking me out on a date?* I clutched at Stevie who suppressed a yelp. "I have an espresso machine in my office. We can go over the party planning milestones and status."

"Oh, right. Right. The party. That would be awesome. I would *love* that." I pumped my fist with enthusiasm.

"Great, I'll have my admin set up the meeting. Looking forward to it."

As soon as he was out of ear shot, I turned frantically to Stevie. "I haven't started a thing! I'm screwed!"

"I'd say." Stevie dragged me away from the coffee bar to berate me in private by the garden. There was an expansive skylight above Gisele's atrium and in the centre was a lush garden of well-groomed and contained botanical wildness. "You are a total Lindsay Lohan hot mess around him. And he loves it! What kind of VP meets with a junior marketer to go over a party timeline?"

"Really? Do you really think he loves me?" I whispered, blushing. The flowers in the garden seemed to bloom brighter.

"For the love of Justin Timberlake, you need to pull it together, girl! This is bad news."

"That's exactly what Calista said!" I knew that Stevie and Calista were soul sisters!

"Who's Calista? You shouldn't be telling people about this! Listen to me. This is a serious CLM. And it needs to stop now." Had I not told Stevie about my best friends? I would have to bring him up to speed on my life outside of Gisele.

The Caden high started wearing off. I felt my heart rate slowing. "You're right. I don't know what comes over me when he's around. I feel totally out of control, like I'm drunk."

"Hmm…OK." Stevie stroked his chin thoughtfully before an epiphany hit him. "I know what we need to do. You need to grow a bigger tolerance to him. Like alcohol. The more you drink, the less it affects you. We'll just find controlled situations to expose you to Caden little by little and eventually you'll work your way up to larger doses."

"I don't know if that's healthy for me." It seemed a little unorthodox but I certainly wasn't going to turn down the opportunity to be exposed to Caden more frequently.

"We'll start with his coffee break." Stevie checked his watch. "I don't know when he takes it, but let's start by meeting here at 10:15 every morning."

"OK." I shrugged. "Let's do it."

Chloe was dodging me like a girl trying to lose a guy after a bad first date. I was going to have to ambush her. I waited around the corner until Chloe returned to her cube. As soon as she sat down I appeared, blocking the entrance.

"Hey Chloe. What's up?"

"I'm busy. What do you want?" Chloe grabbed some random file folders, stood up and assumed face-off position with me. She was wearing a white leather jacket, black jeggings, thigh high black boots and, much to my disappointment, was totally pulling it off.

"Well, I had a conversation with Caden and he was thrilled with how well we're working together. He wanted me to thank you." I smiled sweetly. Her eyes narrowed, suspicious. "I have a meeting with him next week to go over the details of the Gi-Spot party. He asked me to meet with you for transition and to help me get started."

Chloe laughed. "I haven't done a thing for the party so I have nothing to transition or help you with. You're on your own. Now if you'll excuse me, I have a meeting to go to."

Unbelievable. Why would Chloe have allowed me to harass and stalk her for over a week if she had nothing to tell me except to get lost? Unless, as was becoming evident, she enjoyed watching me squirm.

"Super." I moved out of her way and promptly headed over to Stevie's cube.

"What's up, pretty lady?" Stevie greeted me.

"Chloe won't help me with the party and I have no idea how to get started."

"Has she contacted or briefed the agencies yet?"

"No, she says she hasn't done anything yet. You mean like a party planning agency?"

"Oh, sweet pea. You really are on your own. You'll need to contact our event planning agency and our PR agency. As brand managers, we don't actually do anything. We hire agencies to do it for us! Sit down. And take notes..."

Stevie's Caden Tolerance Plan was now in effect. Since Caden didn't seem to have a regular morning coffee break schedule there was a lot of waiting around and drinking coffee. I was developing quite a liking for espresso, perhaps by association. Stevie and I would sit by the edge of the garden, an interesting perspective from which to observe Gisele's culture. There was a clear divide among levels of seniority and associated behaviour.

VPs and Directors used the coffee bar to network with their colleagues (i.e., brag about their successes and complain about work. Their latest beef was Klaus's new rule to only use taxis, and not limos, for business-related transportation). Heidi only appeared with her entourage of Chloe and Jasmine Tit. Their objective was to reinforce their fashion superiority among the junior female marketers. They had nothing on Stevie. Jasmine Tit spoke relentlessly about her boyfriend. I wondered if it was a strategy to keep people away from her entourage. Mateo treated the coffee bar like an actual bar scene. He shamelessly hit on the barista and tried unsuccessfully to break into the Heidi entourage. His persistence was strangely endearing. Sydney saw the bar as an opportunity to obtain approvals and feedback from Savannah, which was quite clever because it was impossible to get into Savannah's calendar. Plus, Savannah only humiliates and beats you down in private.

When Caden did appear, he was often engaged in conversations with other VPs and Directors. The sunlight and garden seemed to brighten in the glory of his gorgeous manliness. Stevie assured me that once I demonstrated normal behaviour in his presence, I would graduate to the small talk stage. Stevie had several drills for me to focus on while in Caden's presence. Deep breathing was a good exercise because it reminded me to breathe. Luckily, my meeting with Caden was delayed a week and a half so this gave me ample time to graduate to an acceptable level.

"You're doing so well!" Stevie congratulated me on the seventh day of the Caden Tolerance Plan. "We're engaging in a coherent conversation. Caden is just a couple feet from you and within eyesight. I think you're close to being able to speak to him – remember stick to the script until you're ready to move on."

I was thrilled – either from the caffeine high or my progress. But there was still an important issue that needed to be addressed.

"Stevie, you and I both know I have a bigger problem."

"Your hands are fine." Stevie assured me. "Small and womanly. Almost as nice as mine." He held up his well-manicured hands to admire them.

"No, no it's my hair. My hair is so unstylish."

Stevie gasped. "I've been so focused on your problem with Caden that I've totally neglecting your appearance. Why don't you get a long bob? A *lob*. So chic."

"I don't know if I can cut my hair that short. I've had long hair my whole life. It would be like cutting off my womanhood."

"Honey, your womanhood is somewhere deep inside you and not in your split ends. Jasmine has great hair. Why don't you ask her where she gets her hair cut?"

When I arrived at the hair studio that Jasmine Tit recommended, I was surprised. It didn't seem like her style, which as far as I could tell, was Euro-snob. Maybe it was her boyfriend's style. It was a whimsical little studio located in the bohemian Queen West area. It was Friday evening and it appeared that I was the last client of the day. Her stylist, Tony, had fat, dirty dreads that matched the rest of his body. He looked like he had had a rough night and hadn't yet recovered. He was certainly rough with me as he washed and combed my hair, yanking my head and hair as if to take out his aggression.

I described the lob cut in excessive Type-A detail, showing him several pictures from magazines that Stevie had given me.

He nodded, bored. "Yeah, yeah, got it. So what brings you here?"

"Jasmine Tit. She said her boyfriend always loves her hair."

"Hmmm…OK. Do you mind if I turn up the music?" He increased the volume to a level where we needed to yell to hear one another.

As he started cutting my hair, he asked me a question. "What?" I yelled.

"If you had to choose a lesbian role model, who would you choose?"

It seemed like an odd icebreaker question. "Uh…I would say Ellen DeGeneres. For sure."

"Who's that?" He screamed in my ear.

"She's a comedian. She has her own talk show." I yelled back.

"I don't own a TV. Tell me someone who's not on TV."

I racked my brain. "Well, there's Dick Cheney's daughter. It must have been hard for her to come out of the closet with her dad in office at the time."

"Who's Dick Cheney?"

A gentle and peaceful looking man entered the studio. "Excuse me. I'm having dinner at the Tibetan Buddhist restaurant just next door. Is it possible to turn down your music? We can hear it and it's disturbing the guests. The owner would never say anything because he's so shy."

Tony stared back at him. "Whatever." He shrugged.

"Thank you. We would greatly appreciate it." He bowed slightly and left.

Tony did not turn down the music and continued to cut my hair. "What a fucking idiot." he spat. I realized he was hacking at my hair and started to get nervous.

"Uh. OK. That's good. Are we done?" I glanced furtively at the door.

"Not even close. I have to razor cut your layers now." Razor cut layers? Is that necessary for a lob?

"Oh! Um, I like it the way it is. Wow, so stylish. It looks awesome."

"Hey relax, I know what I'm doing." He turned down the music. "Is that better?"

"Yeah, I guess." I looked longingly at the exit, fearing that the situation was turning into a potential crime scene. We were the only ones remaining in the studio. He was angry at Tibetan Buddhists and wielding a sharp object. I grew increasingly tense as he continued to hack haphazardly at my hair. There were alarming amounts of hair on the ground. He talked about his recent bi-sexual conquests. It was quite disturbing. I couldn't imagine that Jasmine Tit would tolerate this kind of treatment and environment, no matter how much her boyfriend loved her hair. Tony styled my hair as if I were a rocker in a 80s rock band. I fought back a panic attack. My hands were shaking as I paid. I ran back to my car, relieved to have escaped unscathed.

It was dark in my car so I was unable to examine my hair up close until I got home. I was supposed to meet up for dinner with Lindsay, Jackie and Calista to talk bridesmaid stuff. I screamed when I saw my hair up close in my bathroom mirror. It was worse than I thought. It was a mullet. It was badly styled so I thought that perhaps I could wash it out. I jumped in the shower. Tony had chopped and razored my thick beautiful long locks to nothingness. As I felt how short the top layers where and how thin the long layers were, I panicked.

"Breathe!" I yelled to myself in the shower, clutching at the wall, practicing Stevie's deep breathing technique. How could I be so vain that I would hyperventilate over a bad hair cut? The more I panicked over my hair cut, the more I panicked over the fact that I was panicking over something as stupid as my hair cut. Is this what an existential crisis felt like?

I tried frantically to call and text Stevie but he wasn't answering. I called Lindsay.

"Hey you. What's up? What's wrong? Hey, are you crying?"

"I got a mullet!" I sobbed. "Children are starving in Africa!"

"Oh…" Lindsay was at a loss.

"It's so stupid!" I wailed. "Why am I crying?"

"I don't know. Why don't you just put on a hat?"

"Please forgive me. I'm so sorry." I hung up and fell sobbing onto my bed. Lindsay tried calling back several times but I was so ashamed of my vanity that I couldn't answer or listen to her voice mails.

When Stevie finally called back he was trashed. I could hear pounding music and high-pitched screams in the background.

"My hair!" I wailed. "I'm ugly."

"Good body. Good face. You don't need good hair," Stevie slurred.

"It's a mullet. I look like a lesbian rocker. I look like Joan Jett."

Stevie gasped. "Is Joan Jett a lesbian?"

"Why do I care?" I cried.

"I care, darling. I'll come over tomorrow and fix it. Gotta go! They've started the shots!"

I fell asleep in my clothes after researching hair extensions and world poverty online. When I woke up I didn't remember what happened but felt hung over and dehydrated.

"What happened?" I asked in my morning grogginess. I looked in the mirror and saw Joan Jett, circa 1980, looking back at me. I had ditched my closest friends over a bad hair cut. I didn't recognize myself.

STEVIE WAS SEVERELY hung over the next day and couldn't come over. Instead, he emailed me photos of cute hats and set up an appointment with an outrageously-priced Senior Stylist at Vidal Sassoon. I was convinced that Jasmine Tit had set me up.

I confronted her in her cube first thing Monday morning. Her beautifully coiffed and perfectly cut locks fueled my fire. "So. I got my hair cut."

"How did it go? Why are you wearing a hat?"

I pulled off my hat. She gasped, bringing her hand up to her heart. "What happened?"

"Tony at Forno. He's an asshole. And possibly a homicidal maniac."

"Oh no! No, no, no! I go to see Toné at Fiorio, not Forno." Jasmine Tit seemed genuinely horrified. She had lost her carefully controlled demeanor in the horror of the situation. "This has been a horrible mistake! I should have written it down for you. I just assumed you knew of Fiorio."

"Oh. Shit."

"It's awful." Jasmine Tit whispered, her eyes wide with pity. "I'm so sorry. Please forgive me.

"No, no, it's not your fault. Don't worry about it. I'm getting it fixed later this week." She really needed to pull it together. I was oddly touched by her concern.

"Do you want me to take a photo and ask my boyfriend what he thinks?"

"Uh…no, thanks." I politely declined her offer. Frankly, I was surprised that she even had an opinion before asking her boyfriend.

I took some comfort that in the continuum of superficiality, I was not nearly as bad as Jasmine Tit. Ever since my fit of uncharacteristic vanity, I had been trying to rationalize my reaction. There is nothing better than in times of self-judgment than to lower the bar of comparison. And Jasmine Tit right now made a great bar.

Later that morning, at the coffee bar, I exchanged my greeting and well-rehearsed small talk with Caden. "The party planning is coming along great. Looking forward to our meeting."

"Great. Hey, cute hat. It's a nice look on you." Caden blue eyes twinkled like a diamond princess-cut Tiffany's solitaire.

After Caden left, Stevie and I practically ran over to the garden and hugged in celebration. We were high on caffeine and victory. I had passed with flying colours, coherent and completely in control of my bodily and speaking functions. Sometimes you just have to be pushed to your limit to realize that it really wasn't as bad as you thought.

Chapter 8: Hot and Bothered

THIS WAS IT. THIS WAS D-day. D as in Divine because my big meeting with Caden was scheduled today. I had prepared like an army trainee in Basic Combat Training from the Caden Intervention Plan to my hair, wardrobe and Gi-Spot party planning. Vidal Sassoon had salvaged my hair massacre – my mullet was now transformed into a stylish bob. It was a big change to my look and it took some getting used to but it was really growing on me. It made me look older and more professional. I had chosen an outfit that showcased my body in a classy way that would make Stevie, my fashion Sven Gali, proud – a black pencil skirt, knee high, lace-up black boots, and a form-fitting silk blouse. I looked like I was part of Heidi's entourage.

I would not have made any progress in the Gi-Spot party planning had it not been for Stevie and surprisingly, Sydney. Stevie had explained the process to me and provided a shortlist of agencies of record. He suggested that I speak to Sydney for templates and timelines since she had planned the Forbidden Fruit launch party. Shockingly, Sydney gave me everything I needed.

"Great minds think alike," she said. "That's exactly what I did when I was given the Forbidden Fruit party to plan. Why reinvent the wheel?" While she simply off-loaded files, and didn't spend any time explaining anything to me, I was still impressed by her generosity. This almost made up for her disastrous lack of support at our last Marketing Review. Maybe not everyone was as nasty as Chloe.

I had tossed and turned the night before like the princess on the pea. It seemed like I woke up every hour. At 4:30 am, I got up to beautify myself and painstakingly style my hair and apply makeup, which were still not natural processes for me. I arrived at the office at 6:45 am. One would think that this would have promoted productivity, but unfortunately I was not in prime condition. Exhausted from lack of sleep, I started my espresso runs at 7:00 am. Nervous and increasingly jittery, I filled up on espresso every hour until Stevie arrived, sometimes treating myself to a double shot. Adrenaline and caffeine pumping enthusiastically through my veins, I bounced over to Stevie's cube at 9:05 am.

"Hi! How do I look?" I struck a ridiculous model pose.

"Why so perky?" Stevie looked unenthused. He had a Starbucks cup in hand and had clearly not fully woken up yet.

"I've been here since seven!" I struck another spectacularly bad model pose.

"Don't do that," Stevie advised. "Ever."

"I've had, like, seven shots of espresso! Woo-hoo! I'm ready to go! How do I look? Is this outfit OK? Look, I did my makeup! What do you think? I love my hair. I didn't think I would like it this short but I love it!" I was speaking in rapid-fire phrases without breathing and my voice was weirdly high-pitched.

"Uh-oh. Your meeting with Caden is today." There was trepidation in Stevie's eyes which would have concerned me if I weren't feeling so energized. "I think you should stop drinking espressos immediately."

"I'm fine! Never better! How do I look?" I started but then stopped myself from striking another pose.

"Hyper," Stevie responded, leading me back to my cube. "We need to get some food in your system." He sat me down. As soon as he let go of me, I bounced back up. He sat me back down again. "Stay here, I'll get you water and something to eat."

"But I'm not hungry!" I bounced up.

"Stay!" Stevie said, pointing at my desk chair firmly.

As soon as he left, I ran over to Sydney's cube. We were launch party buddies so that made us work BFFs. It seemed logical at the time.

"How do I look?" I struck a slightly more subtle model pose.

"Fine, except for the stripper heels." As Sydney saw my face fall, she added, "They're not my style. But guys will dig it."

I beamed. "Thanks!" I ran back to my cube before Stevie knew I had left without his permission. But wait a minute – I didn't need his permission to leave my desk. It was time to make some more work BFFs…at the coffee bar!

I skipped over to the coffee bar. Unfortunately, my choice was either Mateo or Heidi's entourage. It was slim pickins. I saw Mateo admiring my stripper heels. I started breaking out into a cold sweat and ran into Heidi's entourage as a means of escape. "Hey guys!" I interrupted Jasmine Tit recounting her boyfriend's opinion of the movie they saw the night before.

The Heidi entourage looked back at me, confused.

"You guys always look *sooo* stylish! Heidi, how do you afford all your gorgeous clothes? Jasmine – I love my hair. Chloe…uh…hi."

Stevie dashed up, rescuing me. "Sorry, ladies. She's had a little too many espressos this morning."

"What were they spiked with?" Chloe asked as Stevie led me away.

"I appreciate that you were trying to make friends, honey, but now's not the right time. Come, I got you some breakfast."

"I'm not scared of them," I proclaimed.

"Good, good. When is your meeting with Caden?"

"Oh my God! What time is it?!"

"It's nine twenty."

"Thank God," I breathed a sigh of relief, "It's at one."

"Good, you have plenty of time…to relax."

"Stevie, do you think my shoes look like stripper heels? I mean, not that that's a bad thing. Just wondering. Wait, no! That is a bad thing."

"No, they're gorgeousness. And you can dress them up and dress them down. What kind of prude told you that?"

"Uh, I would be that prude," Sydney said, approaching us.

"No offense," Stevie said, refraining from a wisecrack.

"None taken," Sydney shrugged. "One man's trash is another man's treasure."

"Hey! These are expensive trash!" I protested, hands on hips.

"Listen, Caden's admin came by looking for you. She wanted to know if you're available at nine thirty. Something came up in Caden's calendar later today."

"Ready? I was born ready!" I did an uncoordinated skip and hop on the spot.

"Are you sure?" Stevie asked. "I think it would be better to reschedule…"

"She looks pretty ready to me," Sydney observed. I was now doing a very uncool sort of hip hop jig on the spot to show off my readiness.

"Sydney, you were so nice to help me with the Gi-Spot party!" I put my hand up to high-five her.

"It's no big deal," she gingerly high-fived me back.

"OK, just please eat something first." Stevie insisted. "I left your breakfast on your desk."

"Thanks! I'm *so* hungry!" I made a mad dash back to my desk.

"Why are you so obsessed with her? Aren't you gay?" I heard Sydney ask as I ran off. "And you definitely can *not* dress down stripper heels."

I HAD BEEN imagining this moment for weeks – behind closed doors with Caden! Be still my maniacally beating, caffeine-overdosed heart.

Caden led me into his sexy lair (OK, it was just his office, but a girl needs her fantasies), placing his hand on my lower back. At his touch, I gasped and jumped up like a high strung cat.

"I'm sorry – you scared the shit out of me!" I exclaimed, somehow making an awkward moment even more awkward.

"No worries. Here, have an espresso," Caden offered further fuel to the fire. Frankly, it would have been rude not to accept. I shot it back, Ronnie style. Caden laughed, perhaps uncomfortably, but at least it helped lessen my high-strung anxiety.

"I'm so excited to finally talk Gi-Spot with you! Yay Gi-Spot!" I exclaimed. *Yay, Gi-Spot?* He laughed again.

"I mean… Gi-Spot party." I laughed nervously.

"Of course, of course. Veronica, it's great to see you so excited. So, how do you like Gisele so far?" He leaned back in his chair and looked me up and down. I felt a little self conscious by his obvious examination but was glad I put the extra hours into getting ready this morning. And for the stripper heels.

"I'm loving it!" I sat down hastily. I indiscreetly scanned his desk for photos of a significant other. Nothing. Yay!

"Veronica, love the hair. It really suits you. Makes you look very sophisticated and older."

"Thanks," I realized I was crossing and uncrossing my legs frantically and stopped suddenly.

He smiled. "So, how's Gi-Spot been going?"

"It's great! And the party planning is great too…" *Uh-oh, was that an inappropriate joke?*

But Caden laughed; oh happy day! I sat up like a proud peacock, thankful for the excessive amounts of caffeine in my system. I would have melted from his hotness by now were it not for the adrenaline.

"I've briefed three event planning agencies and our PR agency. We should be getting proposals by next week. I've also prepared a timeline of key milestones which I can leave with you for review." Desperately in need of oxygen, I stopped to audibly take a deep breath.

"Excellent. No need to review the timelines. You have it all under control. All I ask is for it to be hot. Gi-Spot is edgy and sexy. That's what makes you perfect for the party."

Was that inappropriate for him to say? Who cares! He thinks I'm sexy! Bring on the inappropriateness! Take that Tracker!

I realized that Caden was keenly reading my thought process through my facial expressions, made even more expressive with the energy provided by eight cups of espresso. I immediately stopped grinning like a Cheshire cat.

Caden smiled again. Or perhaps, knowing the effect it had on women, he kept a perma-smile on his face. "Here, I want you to watch something. Gi-Spot UK launched with this 60 second spot during the MTV Europe Awards."

As I watched the TV spot, my excitement turned into slight discomfort. Sexy edge? This was more like porn. It was a little awkward watching soft porn with your VP, particularly if all your G-rated school-girl fantasies of him involved cuddling, holding hands and kayaking, (I figured Caden's rugged good looks would encourage me to embrace the outdoors). The spot ended with a post-coital naked model looking down at the direction of her crotch and then slyly back at the camera, saying, "This is my Gi-Spot. Go find your own."

"What do you think?" Caden asked.

"Uh…" I had absolutely no idea what to say. I felt as prudish as Sydney.

"Pretty hot, huh?"

"Hot and bothered," I agreed. *Is it hot in here?* He raised an eyebrow. *Oops, did I just say that out loud?* Yes, gauging from his face, I definitely just said everything out loud.

He smiled. "Now you have a better idea of what I'm looking for."

I was confused at first. "Oh, you mean for the party! Yes! Totally! Can't wait!"

Caden laughed. "You're funny."

"It's gonna be hot," I promised him. I wondered if he found charity sexy.

"Good, can't wait." He winked at me, making my heart flutter. Or was that the caffeine?

"How did it go?" Stevie showed up promptly at my cube two seconds after I sat down. I was still hot and bothered from my meeting.

"Awesome. But I think I need a cold shower."

"Ew. What happened?"

"We watched porn. It was great."

"Please tell me you're joking." Stevie's face had gone white. Mine was still flushed.

"He showed me the UK Gi-Spot TV ad. It's basically soft porn. He wants the Gi-Spot party to be as hot and bothered as…well, soft porn."

Stevie sighed. "Oh no, he's awful. He has such a bad reputation for hitting on young marketers. Don't let him seduce you." I was outraged at this accusation and didn't want to believe Stevie. Caden may have been slightly inappropriate and did flirt quite frequently but he would never cross the line. Well, depending on which line we're talking about.

"Too late." I felt my coffee high slipping slightly.

"Oh no…" Stevie left me alone with my hot and bothered thoughts. I tried to get work done but I found myself reading the same email over and over again. I was growing increasingly concerned with Stevie's accusation of Caden's inappropriate behaviour with young marketers.

My phone rang. It was Savannah. "Please come see me in my office," she demanded. Uh-oh, did Stevie tell on me?

"Good news," she told me when I arrived, breathless, seconds later. Her Medusa hair seemed calm. The snakes appeared to be napping. "I'm assigning the Phat Lash Mascara launch to you."

My eyes widened in distress. How was I going to plan my hot and bothered party, make women buy ten times more mascara than they need and launch fat makeup at the same time?

"I know. You're welcome," the corners of Savannah's mouth pulled up in a laboured smile. "It's going to be *very* high profile. Phat Lash uses revolutionary new technology. It's enriched with cellulite."

I half laughed and half gasped. "Seriously?"

"I'm sorry? Did I just say something something funny?" Savannah's sharp voice cut short my amusement.

"No," I replied, quickly assuming a serious expression.

Savannah launched into a detailed description but I was distracted by happy thoughts of Caden and me laughing in his office over Gi-Spot puns.

"Veronica!" Savannah shrill voice interrupted my happy place. The Medusa head of snakes stirred. "Pay attention. I'm not going to repeat myself. This product is revolutionary and I want to pay it justice with an innovative launch, not just recycle the US launch plan. I'd like to see your first crack at a go-to-market strategy in two weeks." *Shit.* Clearly, Savannah did not think that sleep was a requirement for me.

As usual, when in distress, I went to go visit Stevie for help. Hopefully he had recovered from my hot and bothered meeting with Caden.

Sydney was in Stevie's cube. They were speaking in hushed voices, which is very unusual for both of them. I heard the words *CLM*, *soft porn* and *espresso addiction* so they were obviously talking about me.

"Stevie, are you dumping me for Sydney because I was cheating on you with Caden?" I joked.

"Dude," Sydney said with her usual poetic tact. "Stay away from Caden or the shit is going to hit the fan."

"Says who?" I challenged.

"I'd give you a few examples but they're no longer at the company," Sydney replied. This was certainly a strange turn of events. Were Sydney and Stevie ganging up against me?

"That's convenient. Give me some credit, guys. I'm not going to do anything." I kind of lied. Sydney crossed her arms, unconvinced.

"Can't a girl lust after a hot executive that she happens to report into without being accused of a CLM?" Stevie and Sydney remained stone-faced and silent. "OK, that didn't sound good," I admitted.

"So are you going to lay off the Caden?" Sydney asked.

"Well, I'm going to be too busy anyway, because I just got assigned some fat mascara launch. And, Savannah wants me to be '*innovative*'." I made air quote gestures for emphasis. "Whatever that means."

"The Phat Lash mascara launch?" Stevie gasped.

"How do you know everything?" I asked in disbelief.

"That's fabulous news!" Stevie exclaimed.

"Yeah, one less thing I have to do." Sydney was relieved to be relinquished from the duty.

"When am I going to find time to do everything?" I moaned. "I need an espresso."

"No!" Stevie and Sydney yelled simultaneously.

Chapter 9: Playboy

IT WAS BECOMING EVIDENT TO me that Savannah's empty diet and social life led to her a constantly angry state. She seemed to live on the brink of collapse on a diet of baby carrots, champagne and contempt for others. She entertained herself by searching for ways to feed the vacant void in her soul by brutalizing others into an equally miserable existence.

Today she summoned me into her office for a 'coaching session'; i.e., closed door session in which she would scold me for my complete incompetence until I admitted my inferiority and begged for emancipation. Her Medusa head of snakes were very active during these sessions and would sneer at me. Then, satisfied with her progress, she would release me from her evil lair so she could continue her sinister plans to join Klaus in world domination. OK, it didn't really happen *exactly* like that…only in my recurring nightmares.

The key learning from this coaching session was that I was not terrifying enough to my cross-functional team members because they actually liked me, which apparently was a bad thing. Indeed, I was not action-oriented enough because I was unable to strike the fear of God into the hearts of my team members. This coaching session was part of my boss's grand plan to brainwash me into thinking the only way to succeed at Gisele was to become her clone, or in other words, the spawn of Satan. Needless to say, this was not a key learning that I would carry with me to Amnesty International.

In addition to my inferiority, I was also left painfully aware that I had not yet started my assignment to wow Savannah with something "innovative" for the Phat Lash launch. As a huge coup to all Gisele marketing peons, Klaus was in Paris representing Gisele Canada with the global powers that be so next month's Marketing Review meeting was cancelled. Luckily, it also bought me more time to find out the secret to revolutionizing mascara usage among Canadian women.

When I returned to my desk, I changed my Facebook status to:

`Veronica is traumatized.`

Seconds later, my phone promptly rang.

"Hey, drama queen," Stevie's voice piped up over the phone. "Snap out of it. I need you to be fun tonight."

I was Stevie's date at a chi-chi gala at the Italian Business Consulate. Stevie was invited because the Gisele fragrances he managed were being sampled in the swag bag. He promised to find me an Italian stallion in exchange for being his date. Italian stallion or not, I was looking forward to being Stevie's date. I owed him several favours and I hoped that this would begin to repay him.

"Oh no, is that tonight?" My heart sank. I had dinner plans with the girls tonight. I had offered to take Lindsay out to make up for my selfish behaviour caused by my lesbian rocker mullet hair cut. It turned out that Lindsay had very little sympathy for sexually ambiguous haircuts and insisted that I treat Jackie and Calista to dinner because my diva behaviour was equally as offensive to them.

Lindsay had already posted a comment to my Facebook status:

`What's wrong? Another lesbian haircut? LOL.`

There was an ominous silence on the phone.

"I have nothing to wear," I decided. It was a half lie – I had picked up a cheap frock at H&M as my rapidly expanding wardrobe was just as quickly leading me into debt.

As Stevie rhymed off a number of expensive options completely out of my price range, I responded to Lindsay's comment on Facebook:

```
Something came up at work. Feel horrible. Rain check?
```

I felt as cowardly as a high school boy breaking up over email.

Stevie's romanticized description of the gala was a far cry from reality. It was actually a networking business event, comprised of questionable Italian businessmen. The guests were uncomfortably donned in formal attire and just as uncomfortably attempting to make polite conversation with their business adversaries.

The average age of our table was eighty. Within minutes of scanning the room, I knew I wasn't going to find my Italian stallion. I resigned myself to a long evening ahead of me, which could only be made tolerable by excessive alcohol intake.

"Whatever you do, don't drink everything that they serve you," Stevie warned me as we sat down at our table. I had promised to be a good date so I obediently but resentfully heeded his warning.

Stevie's advice was only intended for me, because he proceeded to drink the seven rounds of alcohol that was served with each course, plus the ones that I didn't drink. By the time I realized his strategy, it was too late. This resulted in his total inebriation and misperception that the people at our table were actually interesting and fun. He spent the dinner engaged in what appeared to be fascinating conversation while I attempted awkward small talk with a seventy-year-old businessman and his beautiful mute wife.

I wondered whether she simply had no conversational abilities or whether her husband trained her to only say yes, please and thankyou in public. In any case, I didn't care. Within minutes I had established that they were very boring, completely disinterested in me and only present for networking purposes. They were also possibly involved in money laundering.

There were gales of laughter from Stevie's side of the table. Apparently, another one of Stevie's talents was to instantly connect with the most obscure and unlikely people. I tried to join Stevie's conversation but despite the promise of witty entertainment, it was completely incomprehensible to a sober participant.

When the dinner was over, our table was asked to pose for a group photograph. As the strangers assembled into a forced family photo, the photographer referred to me as Stevie's wife. Stevie and I almost burst into raucous laughter but, mindful of our surroundings, we quelled our hysteria and let people believe what they wanted to. When we later saw the photo, Stevie and I were the only ones smiling in a group of somber, stiff Mafiosos.

As if the evening couldn't get any worse, I saw Mateo approach who, judging from the way he walked, had also consumed all seven rounds of alcohol.

"Hey Mateo." I accepted my fate as I had nowhere to run. The eighty-year old Mafiosos and Stevie had just hit the dance floor.

"Hey Veronica," he pronounced my name with a Spanish accent. "You look almost as beautiful as Heidi tonight."

"Uh…thanks?" I wasn't aware that Heidi was the epitome of beauty but was not surprised that the high-end escort look was appealing to Mateo.

"Dude, I got it bad." He slumped down, uninvited, beside me. "Heidi's the hottest girl in the world. She makes Miss America look fake."

"Mateo, I had no idea you had a thing for Heidi!" His behaviour certainly did not support that he had his sights set on one woman, much less Heidi. But hey, he was drunk, and the truth serum was talking. "How do you know you don't have a chance?" He had no chance in hell.

"I just have to work up the nerve to approach her when she's alone. But she always has those two chicks around her and they're as scary as Russian gymnasts." He had a point. Maybe they weren't mean. Maybe they were just hungry and malnourished. "I try to get her to notice me by hitting on other chicks."

"I don't understand your logic." Perhaps it was silly to attempt to understand an illogical man's logic, but he was pouring his heart out to me and I took pity on him.

"Cause all girls love bad boys. And playboys. Like me."

"Not all girls love playboys," I advised. "Why don't you just talk to her?"

"OK, tell me which line I should use: Are your feet tired? Cause you've been running through my head all day."

"Seriously? Do you really think that's going to work?"

"How about this one: Can you give me a Band-Aid? I hurt myself falling for you."

"No. Absolutely not."

"There's 200 bones in the body but baby you give me —"

"Stop! That's disgusting. Just talk to her – like a normal person."

He looked back at me blankly so I offered a suggestion. "Try this line: Hi, how are you? You look nice today."

"That's never going to work," Mateo scoffed.

"Have any of your lines ever worked?"

"Fine. But if she disses me, I'm hitting on you next." Mateo pointed his finger at me and pulled the trigger, as if it were a gun.

"No! I do not agree to that!" I yelled as he loped off to cut a rug on the dance floor.

"Veronica, I didn't know you would be here tonight." There was a flash of brilliance brought on by Caden's beauty, or maybe it was his teeth. It looked like he had just re-whitened them. My stallion had finally appeared!

"I'm Stevie's date!" I exclaimed, instantly reduced to a giggly school girl.

"His date?" Caden looked like he was searching for words to delicately explain the obvious to me.

"Oh no, it's not like that. Stevie's my gay boyfriend."

Caden looked even more confused.

"He's like my gay BFF. Totally platonic. You know, every girl has a gay boyfriend, or at least they should."

"Huh, well, I learned something new tonight." We smiled at each other. Was I actually having a normal conversation with him without drooling, panting or stuttering? I was making real progress!

What only Mateo would describe as a gorgeous woman approached, her large, fake boobs perkily positioned. She looked like the poster girl of high-end prostitute style.

"Hey babe, do you have a gay boyfriend?" Caden asked her, putting his arm around her waist. My smile and all colour melted from my face as I watched the scene unfold in front of me in horror.

"I hope you're not gay," she responded, draping herself all over him like a dirty rag. I felt like the wind was knocked out of me.

"Veronica, this is my girlfriend Britney."

"Hi," I croaked without offering my hand to shake.

"Caden, should I be worried that you work with all these pretty high school girls?" Britney pouted. She was nauseating. What did he see in her? The last time I was around this much plastic was, well, at Gisele…

"You have nothing to worry about," Caden reassured his plastic girlfriend. "Veronica's taken." He pointed at Stevie, clearly not understanding my gay boyfriend explanation. By Britney's expression, even she could tell that Stevie was gay.

I felt like a wilted flower. I didn't have the energy to explain my relationship with Stevie or my educational history so I weakly excused myself to go find Stevie.

I passed by the dance floor where Mateo was trying to heat it up. He was reinforcing the stereotype that white men have no rhythm, blissfully unaware of how ridiculous he looked among the eighty-year old couples trying to waltz. I stopped for a moment to watch his running man transition into the robot. I hoped for his safety that he wouldn't try any of his lines on the women at this event. Except Britney. That would be funny.

I found Stevie at the bar, who was hitting unsuccessfully on the bartender. Apparently, alcohol impedes the effectiveness of Stevie's gay-dar. The bartender was very straight.

"Stevie." I saved the bartender. "Caden has horrible taste in women."

I looked morosely at Caden and Britney. She was still hanging shamelessly off of him. Her boobs were probably throwing her off balance and she needed the support.

"And you have horrible taste in men," he responded.

"What's the dirt on Britney?" I continued to watch them, eyes narrowed and arms crossed. She was chewing at his ear. Ew. She made Mateo look classy. "How long is she going to last?"

"Who cares? I've never seen him with the same woman twice, but they all look the same. Like a dumb Barbie doll. He's such a cliché."

Game on bitch, game on. Hmm, I could dye my hair blonde but getting a boob job to land Caden was a little excessive.

"You're pathetic. You know what I'm going to do tomorrow?" Stevie stepped unsteadily in front of me to block my view of the disgustingly intimate couple. "I'm reporting you to HR."

Mateo approached, a welcome interruption, oddly enough.

"Hey Mateo, why don't you try one of your lines on Caden's girlfriend? You can see firsthand that they don't work." It was worth a shot.

"Oh, they work baby," he assured me.

"Matthew's a playboy," Stevie put his arm around Mateo and then retreated when he felt that Mateo was drenched in sweat. Even in a drunken state, Stevie was excessively hygienic. He excused himself hastily, in search of baby wipes.

"Hey, what I told you before. It's between you and me. Don't tell Stevie." Mateo asked.

Why on earth would Mateo choose me of all people to confide

in? “No worries.” I said. Besides, if Stevie knew, he would probably launch a campaign to hook them up and the whole company would know, which would embarrass Mateo even more when Heidi inevitably rejects him.

“So, how long have you been in love with Caden?” Mateo asked.

I was taken aback. “Is it that obvious?” I realized that I was staring, laser-focused, at Caden and Britney.

“A playboy knows.”

“I won’t tell if you don’t.” I offered. It was now clear why Mateo chose me to confide in, other than my sage wisdom.

“Say it.” He demanded.

“Say what?”

“You know…”

“Fine. You’re a playboy.”

We leaned against the bar watching the gross couple. “Sorry babe, but you know you don’t have a chance in hell with him.” Mateo mopped his brow with a bar napkin.

“I know,” I admitted.

“You’re way to classy for him. What do you see in him anyway? He’s a douche bag.”

“What do you see in Heidi?” I changed the subject.

“She’s the perfect woman,” he shrugged.

“So when are you going to make your move?”

“I don’t know. Is there an app for that?”

“I wish,” I answered as I watched Caden and his prostitute girlfriend leave the event.

Chapter 10: Desperate Heathen

With mounting panic at the desperateness of my situation, I had been gorging my brain with all the mascara research we've done in North America to find a needle in a haystack: how to get women to buy multiple mascara products at the same time. It was like Mission Impossible except without all the cool spy stuff and Tom Cruise. Stevie and his new partner in crime, Sydney, appeared at my cube, arms crossed.

"What?" I was instantly suspicious. Why else would Stevie bring reinforcements?

"We're setting you up on a blind date," Stevie informed me.

"I have no time," I responded, blowing them off. "Klaus and Savannah want me to revolutionize the mascara industry and I'm having revolutionist block."

"Speaking of revolutionize – you revolutionized your fashion style and now we're going to help you revolutionize your love life." Stevie said with the credibility of a late night infomercial.

"You have no choice." Sydney stepped in to close the deal. "There's no backing out."

"I appreciate the concern, but absolutely not."

"You really need to get out more. Come on, it'll be fun." Stevie encouraged me. It was a poorly guised effort to save me from my pathetic crush on Caden and my doomed trajectory towards a CLM.

"I'll do it on one condition – only if you help me revolutionize the mascara industry."

"I know exactly what to do," Sydney said. "But I'll only tell you if you go on the date."

I didn't know whether Sydney was bluffing but decided it was worth a one-hour drink to find out.

"Fine, but only because I'm desperate for help on transforming the face of mascara marketing and not because I'm desperate for a date."

SYDNEY AND STEVIE had sworn on Justin Timberlake's hotness that they were not setting me up with a psycho killer and that I would not end up bludgeoned to death by the end of the date. They were also generous enough to show me a photo of Mark to help identify him. I was encouraged. He looked decent.

However, any positivity I had built up for the date quickly dispelled when I met him face to face at The Beaconsfield, one of my favourite Queen West bars and the only saving grace of this set-up. I saw Mark sitting nervously at the bar. He was my height and looked like a white version of Shrek.

"Mark?" My disappointment must have been written all over my face.

"Yes, are you disappointed?" he asked, giving Mateo a run for the Worst Line Ever award. Any guy whose first words were *are you disappointed* probably had a pretty consistent track record of disappointing women. I felt bad for him. But I was still going to give Stevie and Sydney a serious ass kicking.

"No," I lied. I noticed his extraordinarily small hands and felt worse for him. Beware the curse of the disproportionate hands.

"So, what's your story?" I asked.

"What did Sydney tell you?" Mark looked panicked.

"Nothing. Why?"

"Oh, good." Mark breathed a sigh of relief. "Not that I have anything to hide."

My eyes widened. There was a broad spectrum of "I have nothing to hide" that ranged from "I'm a big Céline Dion fan" to "I eat babies for breakfast."

"Well, it's just that I broke off my engagement with my fiancée a few months ago and you know, things have been a little tough since then."

"Oh," I said, motioning the bartender over so I could start drinking immediately.

"I'm Jewish and it turns out that she didn't want to raise our kids Jewish. That's a real deal breaker for me."

Oh happy day, he was graciously offering me an out! "I'm not Jewish," I told him.

"I've since become more flexible with my beliefs. The biggest deal breaker is that she lied to me about it throughout our whole relationship."

"I understand. I lie to impress guys all that time." That did not appear to faze Mark so I asked, "What do you do for a living?"

"I'm in debt." He saw the look on my face and clarified. "I assess debt for a living. And, well, I guess it's kind of fitting because I'm also in serious credit card debt, which is why I moved into my dad's basement."

Stop talking. Now. The bartender served me my drink. I ordered another one right away. I had promised Sydney and Stevie that I would make an effort to stay an hour and it was feeling like that may be an impossible task.

"It's only temporary," Mark assured me as I gulped my drink back ferociously. "But enough about me. What about you?"

"Nothing much. I'm pretty boring. I work with Sydney at Gisele and that's my life. All work and no play. "

"I think it's impressive how ambitious and driven you are," he flinched.

"Then why did you just flinch?" I called him on it.

"Oh, I have Tourette's. I pretty much have it under control with the medication and all but when I'm really nervous, I blink my eyes a lot." He blinked.

"I'm sorry." Apparently looking like Shrek wasn't his only physical handicap. I checked my watch. Forty-five minutes to go. Forty-five agonizing minutes before I can kick Sydney's ass.

"Mark! Hey there! Fancy running into you here!" Two guys approached us at the bar, taking turns with Mark doing a very bad impression of acting surprised.

"Why don't you join us?" Mark suggested after the awkward introductions. They insisted on leaving us lovebirds alone and sat one table over, within ear shot.

"Did you tell them to show up so that they could listen in on our date?" I asked. His friends got up and moved over to the other side of the room.

"No," Mark blinked.

"Look, you're a really nice guy, but this isn't working out." I said. He looked so crushed that I took pity on him and spent the remaining forty-five minutes giving him advice on how to conduct himself on a first date. After all, I was getting the Holy Grail of mascara marketing after this date. At least he can get something out of it, too.

The truth was I wasn't going to kick Sydney's ass, not only because she could probably inflict serious injury on me, but also because she was saving my ass with her help on my impossible mascara assignment.

"How did it go?" Sydney asked the next day at work.

"Do you really have to ask?"

"OK, I admit, it wasn't my best set-up but we had to do something quick to distract you."

"Next time, come up with a better distraction. OK, so spill the goods. How do we revolutionize the mascara market?"

"Research," she answered. I waited with bated breath for her to go on, but she didn't.

"That's it?" I started calculating how much espresso I needed to drink to build up the courage and energy to actually kick her ass.

"Yeah, if you don't know, you need to gather up mascara-obsessed women and speak to them in focus groups. Find out what insecurities are driving their purchases and then try to make everyone else as equally insecure."

"That seems so obvious. Why didn't Savannah just tell me to do that?"

"Because she wants to see you sweat." Sydney said. "Trust me." Something in her voice told me that Sydney once lost a lot of sweat to offer me this piece of advice.

"Thanks," I said, truly grateful for the sweat that Sydney saved for me.

It was Saturday afternoon and I was trying unsuccessfully to assemble an Ikea entertainment unit I had purchased months ago. The box had been put to good use as a TV stand and shelf and probably would have continued as such. However, I was finally having my girls over for dinner tonight to redeem myself and I wanted to show them that even though I may act like one, I was not living like a heathen. I had spent the whole day cleaning up my heathen-like ways, realizing that sadly, the exercise may take longer than a day. There was a knock at my door.

Oh no – could my neighbours hear me cursing and throwing Ikea parts around in frustration?

I answered the door, mystery Ikea part in hand.

"Hi, I'm Will. I live next door." He had an effortless just-rolled-out-of-bed-but-not-a-pothead look about him that probably took a lot of thought and effort to put together.

"Oh right, I recognize you from around. I'm Veronica."

"Cool. I'm in a band and we're going to be practicing in my condo on the weekends – only during the day. I'm just checking whether that's OK with my neighbours first."

"Depends on how good you are." He paused, not knowing whether I was joking or serious. "I'm kidding. I usually work on the weekends anyway. But I never hear a thing so you shouldn't have a problem."

"Great, thanks. Hey, do you like punk?" he asked.

"Uh, apparently. I've dated a few in the past."

He laughed. "We're playing at the Rivoli next month if you wanted to check us out. We're called The Enlightened."

"Sure, that sounds like fun." Jackie loved guys in bands. It could be a fun girl's night out.

"Cool. Hey, do you need any help?" I lived in a small box of a junior one bedroom condo. He could clearly see the Ikea bomb that had exploded in my living room.

"Oh, I have it under control." I assured him. I may be naïve but I wasn't going to let a total stranger into my condo, even if I was a desperate heathen and he was the most polite punk rocker I'd ever met.

"Well, let me know if it doesn't work out. I'm a carpenter by day so it's no problem."

"It's all good," I responded, intrigued by the carpenter/punk rock combo. How often does a man come along that both Jackie and Lindsay would approve of?

I HAD GIVEN up on the entertainment centre but did manage to stuff it all back into the box. Lindsay, Jackie and Calista forbade me to complain about work. I was instantly silenced when I tried to ask them their thoughts on revolutionizing mascara use.

"You are not allowed to complain about your job," Lindsay warned me. "It's bad enough that we never see you but now we have to listen to you whine about it when we're with you?"

Other than that, they were really cool about my heathen-like behaviour, partially because my date with Shrek amused them but mostly because they're good friends. My conversational topics vastly limited since I was prohibited to talk about work, I found myself raving endlessly about Stevie, to the point where I even creeped myself out.

We had just finished dinner (which I had picked up pre-prepared from Whole Foods) and Lindsay and Calista were helping me put together the entertainment unit.

"You need to accept that Stevie's gay. If you want to be set up, I have plenty of prospects for you." She was watching us struggle with the Ikea unit, perched on the sofa, drinking wine.

"I don't want any of your loser rejects," I told her. "Finding a good man is as hard as finding your Kegel muscles."

"Kegel exercises are a breeze," Jackie asserted. "I'm doing them right now."

We all turned to look at Jackie as she smiled at us, glass of wine in hand.

"Anyway," I broke the awkward silence. "I might have a prospect for you, Jackie. My neighbour is in a punk band and invited me to his show at the Rivoli next month."

"Why don't *you* go for him?" Lindsay asked. "Jackie doesn't need any help with prospects."

"Don't listen to Lindsay. I'll take whatever I can get." Jackie leaned back on one hand as we continued to struggle with the Ikea unit. "But it is convenient for you that he's your neighbour."

"He's not really my type. But Lindsay, you'd approve of him – he's a carpenter. He offered to put together this unit for me. Assembling this Ikea unit may be as impossible as revolutionizing the mascara industry —"

"Oh, shut up about your stupid job," Lindsay interrupted and started stuffing the Ikea parts back in the box. "Can't you see, Veronica? He likes you."

"Totally." Calista agreed, and joined Lindsay in undoing whatever minimal progress we had made on the entertainment unit. "Inviting you to his show, offering to help you assemble this? He's practically throwing himself at you."

"Let me get this straight – you're not helping me out so that I could invite a strange man into my condo? How desperate am I that I throw myself at the first heterosexual guy that is nice to me?"

"It's not desperate," Jackie said. "It's strategic."

"Well, let's just go to the show and see how it goes," I conceded.

"Oh, and one more thing," Jackie said as she raised her glass. "I'm doing them again."

I WASN'T EXPECTING Savannah to grant me with a Nobel Prize when I recommended that we conduct research with mascara-obsessed women, but I did at the very least expect some sort of recognition that I wasn't a complete failure. In fact, I thought my work may have even been worthy of advancement in Chloe's Tracker.

"Hmm. Did you do a complete scrub of all existing North American research? It's best that we don't waste money duplicating efforts."

"Yes. There were no learnings specific to our objectives of increasing multi-mascara usage but there are some great insights which I've summarized in this report." I handed over the report. This was Stevie's advice to me, in exchange for whoring me out to Shrek.

"Hmm." Savannah seemed at a loss for gut-wrenching insults. Her Medusa head of snakes stirred restlessly for blood. "Well, you just earned yourself a new project. Set up the research. And make it fast. Klaus will be back from Paris soon and we need to give him an answer yesterday." This additional assignment felt more like a punishment than a reward for my resourcefulness. "Now, how's Phat Lash going?"

"I've been focusing on this project so I'm planning on starting the analysis this week," I responded, trying not to let my desperation and panic show.

"What? You haven't started yet? Do I have to hand hold you through every project? Do I have to do everything myself?" Savannah's shrill voice and blood pressure rose with every question she asked.

"No, no," I said, trying desperately to keep my own blood pressure under control. *Why can't I learn to lie to my boss, damn it?* "I'll be done the proposal next week, like you asked."

"No, Veronica, I asked for it to be complete this week," she insisted in a sinister tone, daring me to challenge her. She was wrong but I didn't correct her lest I be raked over the coals for insubordination. One of the snakes stuck its tongue out at me.

"OK, I'll have it done this week," I conceded in weak defeat. It was Wednesday afternoon. If I had balls, they'd be shrunk to nothingness at this point.

"Do YOU REMEMBER Joey from the gala at the Italian Business Consulate?" Stevie asked me the next day over lunch.

"No. I thought you were too drunk to remember anything?"

"I'm pretty sure I introduced you. Anyway, he remembers you and has been asking about you."

"I don't remember him. I'm not interested," I said with the decisiveness of someone who still believed that she was not desperate.

"Well he wants to meet you again. He's cute – if you don't mind potheads. And he has a good body...but he's a little on the short side."

I envisioned a midget smoking pot alone in his parent's basement. This was starting to sound familiar.

"He's rich – but he's balding." Essentially, Stevie was trying to set me up with a young Danny DeVito. It was a sobering thought but this was what may be left of Toronto's bachelors.

"If he was so interested, why didn't he make a move at the gala?" I asked. Better to sound skeptical than shallow.

"He was engaged. He just called off the wedding and really wants to meet you!"

"Seriously?" I said, attempting a tone of voice frequently used by Savannah – annoyed that he was wasting my time, disgusted by his stupidity and mildly amused by how pathetic he was. Once I perfected this tone, I would be promoted.

"I know you're way too good for him but doesn't it make you feel better that despite your bad choice in men, there's always someone worse? And by bad choice in men, I mean Caden."

"Thanks, I guess that's one way of looking at it." Stevie understood the female psyche well. Better to be delusional of your superiority than self-pitying in your loneliness.

"Despite what you think, there are people other than me who think you're hot. By the way, did anyone tell you that your shoes are fierce? Your skin is glowing and your hair is fab!"

"Who needs a boyfriend when you have a gay friend?" Sydney asked, just joining us. "I don't get that many compliments from my boyfriend in a whole year."

"That's because you put out for him a long time ago," Stevie answered.

Chapter 11: Barren

I WAS ABOUT HAVE MY spirit crushed by Savannah when Celeste, the VP of Hair Colour, stopped by her office and interrupted for a social catch-up, clearly more important than our business matters at hand.

I was instantly suspicious of Celeste. Anyone whose name rhymed with molest was not to be trusted. It appeared that Celeste's face had a fight with Botox and the Botox had won. It must have been a bad one because Celeste's expression had been traumatized into a permanently surprised state. I stared at her perfectly arched motionless eyebrows as she spoke.

"Sorry I missed our cappuccino break this morning," Celeste said. "I got in late because I couldn't sleep last night. I have a meeting with Klaus this afternoon and I've been falling behind my financial targets. The shit's going to hit the fan!"

"I know what you mean. I woke up at 3 am and couldn't get back to sleep!"

Celeste and Savannah laughed at their stress-induced insomnia. Celeste's frozen face strained to laugh. She reminded me of the Bride of Chucky. It looked like her skin might crack and my face hurt just looking at her. I did not find any humour in their situation but it was the first time that I actually felt some sort of empathy for Savannah.

"Veronica's not laughing." Savannah pointed out. "Do you have any trouble sleeping?

"No, I read this really boring book before I go to bed and it knocks me out in less than two pages. I think it's about World War 2."

They laughed hysterically again. "We need something a lot stronger than that to knock us out!"

"Valium!" Celeste screamed.

"Ambien!" Savannah screamed back and their forced hysteria continued. I hoped that my confused expression did not come off as disrespect. I was quite impressed by their command of sedatives.

"Celeste's so funny!" Savannah commented after Celeste left. If by funny she meant tragically sad and over-Botoxed, I would agree. Nonetheless, I was glad that Celeste had left Savannah's head of snakes in a good mood for our meeting. The bizarre exchange somehow made these intimidating women seem real to me. They were just two sad ladies laughing at how sad their lives were. I would try to remember this conversation next time Savannah scares me into shitting my pants.

"I'm sorry if I called you stupid last time we met." Savannah began the meeting.

"That's OK, you didn't call me stupid," I said.

"Really? I'm pretty sure I did. Well, it must have been someone else, then. In any case, you're doing a good job so it pissed me off when you screwed up."

"I'm sorry," I responded in the hopes of keeping her head of snakes calm. This meeting was getting increasingly bizarre. Maybe Savannah really was bipolar and her drugs were finally kicking in.

Hopefully, she was also partially sedated. My efforts over the past couple of late nights had not revolutionized mascara marketing but was, as Stevie assured me, a solid recommendation for the Phat Lash launch based on what traditionally works in the Canadian market.

"Hmmm," she said when I finished speaking. In general, "Hmmm" was not a good sound coming from Savannah. It roughly translates to "you poor pathetic idiot" and usually preceded a snake lashing.

"I'm not going to call you stupid again but I'm surprised you haven't incorporated anything like Facebook or Twitter." Social media was Gisele's new corporate obsession. The world was changing and Gisele needed to be where the money was. "Or even some sort of a charity element, what with your not-for-profit background. Think about it and come back when you actually have a good idea."

Savannah was clearly sedated because she let me off relatively easy but she was right about the charity element. I couldn't believe I didn't think of that. The world was changing but I wasn't.

STEVIE HAD INVITED me to join him and his latest love interest, Jamie, for a Friday night dinner at Lee, one of Stevie's favourite restaurants. After the last week of slave labour, I didn't know what I needed more – excessive amounts of sleep or alcohol. Stevie was shocked that I even needed to think about it. Alcohol, of course.

"Veronica, finally we meet! I've heard so much about you!" Upon introduction, Jamie seemed like a lovely boy and thus good enough for Stevie.

"So good to finally meet you too!" I said, pointedly looking at Stevie. I hadn't heard anything about Jamie until this dinner invitation. "I don't know why Stevie has kept you a secret for so long."

"I haven't shared a lot about Jamie, because of, you know, your situation." Stevie said.

"What's my situation?"

"You know, barren."

"Barren?" I practically spat. Stevie was really getting aggressive about his lack of approval of my infatuation with Caden.

"I wouldn't say barren is accurate," Jamie jumped in to save me. "That makes her sound infertile, or without child."

"No, barren like a desert. No life or vegetation," Stevie insisted.

"OK guys, can we talk about something else?"

"It's tough love, girlfriend. All work and no play makes Ronnie a dull girl." Stevie turned to Jamie. "We offered to set her up but my Ronnie has high standards," Stevie winked at me. "She has a thing for man whores."

"I don't know why such a beautiful girl like you is single. I know plenty of guys that would die to date you." Jamie offered.

"Are they straight?" I asked.

"I'll have to get back to you on that," Jamie said after a pause.

The dinner went well after I started consuming excessive amounts of alcohol and the conversation moved away from my lack of a love life. I thought Stevie and Jamie made a cute couple when they weren't discussing my barrenness.

I also learned more about Stevie and his aspirations to start his own fashion police company.

"Stacy and Clinton from *What Not to Wear* are my idols," Stevie said. "I aspire to carry on their legacy. Look what I've done with Veronica. She was a fashion tsunami before I got my hands on her."

"You are a master," I agreed. I felt like I belonged with Lee Restaurant's fashionable yuppies in my Stevie-approved outfit – skinny jeans, horribly uncomfortably high heels and a belted boyfriend blazer.

"I believe that with the right coaching, everyone has the ability to make good fashion choices. Fashion sense is like a muscle. It's all within us – it just needs to be trained," Stevie mused. If fashion were a muscle, Stevie would be an Olympic weight lifter.

"Thank God Stevie met the right coach a long time ago." Jamie smiled.

"What's this?" I perked up.

"It's true," Stevie admitted. "I was almost as bad as you. When I saw your harem pants, I saw myself five years ago in leather pants and a cropped acid wash jean jacket."

"Ew," I said. "*Almost* as bad as me? That's horrific."

"So how much do you love Jamie?" Stevie asked me the next Monday at our coffee break by Gisele's lush garden. "Everyone loves him. He's like Miss Congeniality everywhere he goes."

"Jamie's great – I'm really happy for you but can you please not call me barren? It's disturbing."

"Oh, it's all in good fun. You're barren by choice so I'm just trying to light a fire under your well-dressed ass. Love those pants, girl!" I had splurged on beautifully-tailored skinny pants from TNT, The New Trend, on the weekend. TNT carried Stevie's favourite over-priced designer lines. If I had a trust fund and Stevie had his way, I would only shop at TNT.

"Why have you been hiding Jamie for so long? He's lovely." I asked.

"I just…didn't know whether it would last, so…um…" Stevie shifted uncomfortably and stuttered uncharacteristically.

"Why wouldn't it? He's fabulous, just like you."

"I'll tell you later," Stevie said as he saw Sydney approach us.

"Hey, are you guys talking about me again?" Sydney joined us with her usual order of *Eiscafé*.

"No, Stevie thinks I'm barren," I told her, knowing she would get a kick out of it. Sure enough, she laughed appreciatively.

"I don't know what you see in that man," Sydney sat down beside us at the garden and we observed Caden in action at the coffee bar. "How can you trust anyone that smiles that much?"

I shrugged. "I would smile that much if I were that hot."

"He's so *tanned*," Sydney shook her head. "Crushin' on your boss. You are such a cliché."

All this talk of barrenness was starting to get to me. "Well, there *is* potentially someone – my neighbour. He seems cool – he's a carpenter and plays in a band."

Sydney and Stevie perked up, like Caden's girlfriend's fake boobs. "Do tell! Is he cute?" Stevie asked.

"I guess so…" I said.

"You don't seem that into him," Sydney observed.

"I just don't think he's my type…but I should at least give him a chance, right?"

"Not if you're not feeling it," Sydney said as Stevie said, "Go for it, girl!" They looked at each other.

"Well, maybe wait and see…" Stevie said as Sydney said, "Well, give it a try…"

"Why don't you guys discuss and get back to me on that?" I suggested and went back to staring wistfully at Caden.

I COULDN'T GET barren images of deserts and empty wombs out of my mind so I decided to take matters into my own hands with Carpenter Man and invite him over to assemble my Ikea unit. I tidied up my apartment by stuffing dishes in the oven and clothes under my bed, and then brushed my teeth by gargling with mouth wash. Stevie would be horrified by my lack of hygiene. I knocked on Will's door.

A man similar in look and age to Will opened the door. He was fresh out of the shower with a towel around his waist. But he was not Will.

"Oh, sorry, I was looking for Will. I'm from next door…I guess I have the wrong condo…" I said, trying not to stare at his nicely-cut chest and abs.

"Will just stepped out for a bit, do you want me to let him know that you stopped by?" he asked politely. I had a mini-panic attack in the span of two seconds. OMG, is he Will's lover? He's *way* too polite and well-kept to be a twenty-something straight man.

"Uh…are you his roommate?" I asked.

"No, didn't he tell you about us?"

"I'm sorry! I'll just come back later," I stammered and took off before Naked Towel Boy could respond.

Lindsay, Calista and Jackie thought I was jumping to conclusions about Will and concocted several far-fetched explanations for Naked Towel Boy, such as a visiting cousin or a friend who was broke and needed a place to crash. To their exasperation, I claimed that there was only one person who could crack the "Didn't he tell you about us?" code.

"Stevie, can a man be gay if he's a carpenter and in a punk band?" I asked as he joined me for a quick lunch by the garden the next day.

"How can you be so stereotypical?" Stevie sighed in exasperation as he set aside his Louis Vuitton bag and neatly crossed his legs.

"Sorry, but I think my only potential boy prospect may be gay… could you check him out? You have such finely tuned gay-dar."

"Ronnie, you know that flattery will get you everywhere with me. I'd be delighted to help you."

"Good. I hope you don't mind punk music – we're going to watch his band play at the Rivoli." Stevie shuddered as if he saw a fake Gucci bag. "Speaking of cute boys, how's it going with Jamie?"

Stevie started to shift uncomfortably and mumble. "Well, it's going really well …" he trailed off.

"Sooo…that's a good thing," I encouraged. I had never seen Stevie so insecure. He must really like Jamie. The level of insecurity you feel in a relationship is highly correlated to the amount that you like the person. It's like a scientific equation.

"Yeah…" he shrugged and picked a non-existent piece of lint of his pants. I felt like I was trying to drag Stevie into Wal-Mart to shop for clothes.

I saw Mateo approach Heidi at the bar, unusually alone. Quite unexpectedly, she didn't slap him. Was Mateo using my advice?

"Look!" I said, smiling in the direction of the coffee bar. It appeared that Heidi and Mateo were engaging in a grown-up conversation that involved smiling and nodding. Very positive body language! I couldn't wait to find out what they were talking about.

"What is it?" Stevie asked. I remembered Mateo and I had sworn each other to secrecy. I felt an odd kinship with Mateo so instead I pointed out Heidi's shoes.

"Fabulous," Stevie agreed, relieved for the change of conversation.

I RAN TO Mateo's cube after lunch to congratulate him. "I saw you and Heidi at the coffee bar – you did great!" I high-fived him.

"It took two weeks for me to make my move. I was stalking her at the coffee bar, it took forever for her to be alone."

"I'm dying to know – what did you say?"

"The first thing that came to my mind: *Do you come here often?"*

I paused.

"She had the same reaction as you! So I said *just kidding* and she laughed."

"Were you kidding?" I asked.

"Nah," he answered.

"Well, whatever works," I laughed.

"I would have never made a move if it weren't for you," he said.

"Really?" I asked, flattered.

"Yeah, whenever I started thinking I didn't have a chance, I just thought of you and your crush on Caden and it gave me hope that at least I had a better chance than you."

"Oh," I said. "Not so flattered anymore."

"Seriously, thanks for your advice. It really helped." He man-hugged me awkwardly, bumping his shoulder to mine and patting me on the back. He suddenly sprung back, his face panicked.

"What's wrong?" I asked.

"She saw me hug you," he whispered.

"Are you sure?"

"Yeah, she stopped by to say something to me and saw us hugging and then just kept walking." He looked devastated.

"It was a man hug! Tell her it was nothing." I said.

“No, no, she won’t believe me,” he slumped down in his desk chair, head in hands. “How could I screw it up before it could even be screwed up?”

“Don’t worry, Mateo, I’ll go talk to her.”

I’m not sure what possessed me to get involved but Mateo’s desperate unrequited love struck a chord with me. I knocked on Heidi’s cube door. “Can I come in?”

“Sure,” she frowned, on guard.

I sat down in the spare chair beside her desk. “Look, Mateo has a huge crush on you. It’s really sweet and I think you should give him a chance.”

“Who’s Mateo?” she asked.

“Oh, sorry, I mean Matthew.”

“Oh,” she said. She played with a section of her hair. “Yeah, he’s nice but…I don’t really think he’s my type.”

“Well, for what it’s worth, he thinks you’re the most beautiful girl in the world and he would treat you like a princess. Isn’t that what any girl would want?”

She looked back at me, silent.

“Think about it,” I said. As I left her cube, she sat quietly, still playing with her hair.

Chapter 12: Intervention

"You were right," Heidi appeared at my cube, espresso in hand. Her hair and makeup were less overdone and much more appropriate for one not involved in the sex trade.

"Right about what?" Heidi appeared to be speaking to me as if I were her fashion equal. Was my outfit that fabulous or had hell frozen over?

"Matthew's a sweetheart," she whispered. "He's totally different from anyone I've ever dated before. He's actually…*nice* to me."

"Oh good, you gave him a chance. How did it go?"

"Good. This is for you." She handed me the espresso. Was I that notorious an espresso aficionado that even Heidi knew my vice? "I've been pretty horrible to you and just wanted to say thanks."

"You're welcome," I graciously accepted the espresso. This was my fourth one of the morning and frankly, it would have been rude to turn it down. "You were only mean to me that one time you laughed at my ugly outfit."

Heidi blinked. "Oh, we always laugh at you behind your back."

"Yeah…that's probably not necessary for you to share with me."

"Please don't tell anyone about Matthew and me," Heidi requested. Ah, of course. Here was the ulterior motive.

"No worries," I told her. "Your secret is safe with me."

"Let me know if there's anything I could do for you. Are you single? I could set you up with someone."

"That's all right." I was still recovering from my date with Shrek and certainly did not trust Heidi's judgment in men. She would probably set me up with a drug lord or porn producer. "I'll think of another way you can pay me back." It was a joke. Sort of.

After guzzling my espresso, I dashed over to Mateo's cube. "How's my favourite playboy? How did it go with the Heid-ster?"

"You're the best wing man ever," he whispered.

"It's no big deal," I said. "You didn't tell her about Caden, did you?"

"No, you can trust me," Mateo answered. "I owe you big time."

I almost answered that he didn't owe me anything but stopped myself. Having these two people owe me favours might come in handy later.

"Please don't tell anyone about Heidi and me," he continued in a whisper. "She's kind of weirded out about dating someone at work."

"Your secret is safe with me. So you guys are dating now?" I dropped my voice down to a stage whisper.

"Well, we've been on a few dates so I guess so…"

"A few dates? It's only been a week!"

"How do I keep this going? What's your advice, Wing Man?" he asked.

"Just keep treating her like the princess that she is," I assured him.

"I wouldn't have it any other way for my Heidi," he grinned. "I'm a changed man, Ronnie."

It was a little couple-in-love gross but it was also kind of sweet. I smiled to cover up my wistfulness. I didn't know what was more surprising to me – the fact that Heidi actually liked Mateo or the fact that I actually envied what they had.

"Just…don't dance in front of her…" I advised.

Heidi did not lose sight of my seminal actions that gave birth to her secret love. She continued to faithfully feed my coffee obsession.

This did not go unnoticed by Stevie and Sydney.

"Holy Justin Timberlake!" Stevie exclaimed after Heidi greeted us at the coffee bar with my ubiquitous espresso. Jasmine Tit took that opportunity to inform everyone at the bar that her boyfriend also loved espresso. It was my seventh of the day. "You should be swinging by the chandeliers by now."

"I've learned to control the adrenaline rush," I delicately sipped my espresso as we headed over to the garden. I had grown fondly accustomed to my racing heart rate and mile-a-minute speech. "But frankly, they'd be a lot better with a shot of Jäger, don't you think?"

"You're addicted," Sydney said.

"No, I can stop any time I want," I retorted. "I only drink socially."

"Not the Jäger, I meant the coffee."

"I don't drink anymore coffee than anyone else," I answered, growing irritated.

"What Sydney's trying to say," Stevie jumped in with an annoyingly gentle voice, "Is that we care about you and we're concerned for your health. We want to help you. Help us help you."

"What is this? An intervention? It's freakin' coffee! Get over it!" I was surprised by how quickly my defensiveness rose. "I mean, it's not like I'm on drugs."

Stevie and Sydney nodded sympathetically, seemingly unsurprised by my dramatic reaction, which irritated me even more.

"Caffeine is like denim on denim," Stevie explained to me slowly as if I were a child. "Too much of a bad thing is not only harmful to yourself, it's *offensive* to others."

"I would never, repeat, *never* wear denim on denim." I affirmed.

"It starts with a great pair of jeans. Then you start wearing them too much. Sometimes even two days in a row." Stevie shuddered. "The next thing you know, you've added a jean jacket."

Sydney put a hand on my shoulder. "It's time you put away your jean jacket."

"Says who?" I asked.

"Says Google." Stevie had me there. One couldn't argue with the sanctity of Google.

"What's up with Heidi? She's like your coffee pimp. Is she trying to sabotage you?" Sydney asked.

"No, she's just being nice," I said. "She only brings me one a day."

"Why so nice?" Sydney crossed her arms suspiciously.

"Maybe she's just a nice girl. Can't someone be nice without having an ulterior motive?"

"I'm on to you Ronnie," Sydney did not believe in niceness for nothing. "Something's up and you're blackmailing her."

"Let's get back to the coffee," Stevie thankfully interjected. "Just try drinking a few less a day, sweetie."

"Fine. As long we never have this ridiculous conversation again," I conceded.

"Good, I'm glad you agree. Now there's one other small issue we wanted to address…" Sydney continued. "It's your obsession with Caden. It's out of control."

"What do you mean? Can't I secretly lust over my boss in peace?" So maybe I constantly searched his name on Google and maybe I was unable to participate in a conversation whenever he was in the same room because I would be concentrating on lip reading his conversation, and maybe I nudged people out of the way at the coffee bar or in the halls or in a meeting to say hi to him. But that's normal behaviour when you have a little crush, isn't it?

"I don't know if it's so secret…" Stevie tried to put delicately. "You'd have to be deaf, dumb and blind not to notice that you're Lady GaGa over him."

"I'm not hurting anyone. It's fun. You guys make fun of me and call me barren. You laugh. I cry. In private. It's our thing."

"It is pretty funny how pathetic you are," Sydney admitted.

"But you're hurting your career," Stevie added.

"No…it makes me work harder because I want to look good for

him." I countered. "So I'd argue that it's actually great for my career."

"OK, sweetie, if you say so." Stevie still looked worried. "Just please try to be less Lady GaGa about it."

"I'm sorry, I'm not fully fluent in gay yet."

"Just be less friggin' obvious about it," Sydney translated in her usual tactful loveliness. "And stop dressing so slutty. Just because his girlfriend's a slut doesn't mean *you* have to dress like one."

"Fine," I pretended to be grumpy about it but the Caden intervention alarmed me. I thought my crush was discreet but how humiliating if it came off as tacky as denim on denim.

After the coffee intervention, I had arranged a bitch session with my girls over drinks after work at the Windsor Arms Hotel, just a few blocks from where I worked. I was hoping for solidarity and a shrewd counter-attack. They didn't offer either. Instead they were confused at the denim analogy.

"What's wrong with denim on denim?" Lindsay asked. "It was my favourite outfit in grade seven."

"Exactly!" I said.

"How can denim be compared to an addiction?" Calista asked.

"Speaking of hot guys," Jackie jumped in, clearly indicating that she wasn't listening. "How's it going with Carpenter Boy?"

"Carpenter Boy's shackin' up with Towel Boy."

"What? Carpenter Boy's gay?" Jackie was disappointed. "What is it with you and the gays? What are you going to do about it?"

"Nothing if he's gay. I can't cheat on Stevie."

"Right, you're an equal opportunity monogamist," Calista agreed.

"Stevie and his gay-dar are going to check him out at the Rivoli. You guys finally get to meet Stevie!"

"You mean – he'll finally get to meet us." Lindsay corrected.

"I can spot a gay from a mile away. They're the only men who don't stare at my boobs. I'll let you know the deal with Carpenter

Boy," Jackie offered.

"It's ironic that Stevie and Sydney are on an intervention kick with you because we've also been wanting to give you an intervention," Calista said.

You're kidding me. I'm annoyed already. "For what?"

"You're working way too much. We never see or hear from you. We see you maybe once a month and you take forever to get back to us." It seemed like Lindsay had waited a while to vent.

"That's not true," I said, trying to hold my irritation back from growing into full-blown anger. I came here to have a bitch session and now it was turning into a bitch session against me. I started yearning for a Jäger bomb.

"You hate your job but you're letting it suck you in," Calista added. "You spend more time doing something you hate than with people that you care about."

"That's not true." It was frustrating that they didn't understand. I needed their sympathy, not their holier-than-thou advice. "It's just that it's a really busy time because I'm doing two jobs right now. Things will get better after the Gi-Spot party."

"You said things would get better three months ago," Lindsay reminded me.

"Stop making excuses for the Man," Jackie added. "You already do that enough for the guys you date."

I felt like a husband being accused of cheating by his three polygamist wives. They were the ones who convinced me to take this job in the first place.

"I'm sorry you guys don't understand." That was the closest I would come to an apology.

"Just don't let them take advantage of you," Calista said.

"OK, guys that's enough. I feel like I'm being interrogated. I hang out with you to forget about work, so let's just forget about it."

"Ah, you know it's fall when Burberry's in the air," Stevie took a deep breath of the Burberry air as we strolled through the side streets of Yorkville during our lunch hour. It was a completely incomprehensible observation to me. All I saw were wellies, designer bags and trench coats, all of which, incidentally, Stevie was wearing.

"So how's it going with Jamie?" I asked. I knew it was a sensitive topic so I had waited until Sydney was not with us to ask.

"Is this a counter-intervention you're having with me?" Stevie shot back, immediately defensive.

"No, not at all," I assured him, taken aback by his aggressive response. "I'm just curious how your love life's going."

"It's fine," he mumbled, avoiding eye contact.

Uncomfortable with his discomfort, I decided not to push any further. "How long were you and Sydney planning my coffee intervention? Sorry, I didn't mean to overreact – it was just so unexpected. I laughed about it afterwards with my girls."

"I thought I was your girl," Stevie said, pretending to be hurt.

"And I thought I was your girl," I mocked him.

"You are my girl. Well, after Madge and Lady GaGa. You're a strong number three."

"Then why are you so chummy with Sydney? You guys are always ganging up on me. I feel like the third wheel." I didn't know I felt that way until I said it as a joke. But now that I said it, hell yeah! We were like a freakin' tricycle.

"Oh, you're such a jealous lover," Stevie said.

"Do you like your new mistress?" I teased. "Is Jamie jealous of her?"

"Leave Jamie out of this!" Stevie yelled.

We both gasped at his uncharacteristic outburst. Stevie covered his mouth with his hand and stopped in his tracks.

"I'm sorry, I don't know what got into me." Stevie moved his hand from his mouth to his heart. "I guess I'm just a little on edge about Jamie."

“I’m sorry about that. Why?”

“He’s so perfect and I’m so happy, I’m just scared that I’m going to screw it up,” he said. “Like I always do.” It was hard to believe that my perfect Stevie could screw something up.

“You’re incapable of screwing anything up,” I assured him. “The more you think about it, the more it’s going to freak you out. Just stop thinking about it and enjoy being with him.” I was pretty impressed with my advice. If only I could follow it.

“Easy for you to say,” he said.

“I know, I’m full of shit,” I admitted.

“Hey guys!” We were approaching the office entrance and Sydney was just coming out.

“Go away, we’re having a moment,” I said.

“Yeah,” Stevie agreed. “I want to be alone with my girl.” He smiled at me.

“OK lovebirds,” Sydney rolled her eyes. “You freaks.”

Chapter 13: Ruffian and Man Boobs

I HAD BEEN HAVING RECURRING nightmares of being caught ugly in Gisele – both awake and asleep. The night before my performance review I had a particularly intense nightmare.

I'm in a Marketing Review meeting and I have an answer for everything. I am so right that I am cocky. Chloe is there, among the designer suits and they are looking at me in horror. Chloe points at my face and I realize that they are not horrified at their lack of intellectual superiority to me but by my ugliness. I feel my face. The Lego-like acne on my face feels like it is growing. Chloe laughs but the designer suits start screaming and covering their eyes, blinded by my ugliness. They try to run out of the boardroom but they can't find the door. Some lunge under the table in fear and others try desperately to pry the windows open. Oompa Loompa appears in his jester outfit. He jumps up on the boardroom table. Chloe joins him and they start dancing an odd jig, an ode to my ugliness. I see Caden among the chaos and try to call out to him to *love me, please love me* but I can't speak because my teeth are falling out. The screams of horror reach deafening proportions.

I woke up wondering where my friends were in the nightmare.

I paid obsessive attention to my appearance that morning. If I was going to fail my performance review, at least I was going to look fabulous going down in flames. I chose a vibrant green dress, the colour of money.

I was distracted that morning, drinking my espresso, pretending it was my only one of the day.

"Green looks fa-bu on you," Stevie gushed. "You should only wear jewel tones."

"Thanks," I said, my vacant expression as inflexible as Celeste's Botox-ed face.

"What's wrong?" Stevie asked. "You're so boring this morning."

"Sorry, I have my performance review with Savannah and I'm kinda nervous about it."

"Oh, don't worry about it. I have my performance review today, too. You'd be fired by now if they hated you."

"You mean Savannah doesn't hate me?" I was shocked.

"Well, she talks to you doesn't she? And she knows your name. That's a promising sign."

"Not really. If she can identify me that'll make it easier for her to fire me."

"There's nothing to be scared of. A performance review goes like this: you're good at *blah, blah, blah*. You suck at *blah, blah, blah*. And then, you just spend the next year trying to suck less at what you suck at."

"What about what you're good at?" I asked.

"Oh, they don't pay much attention to that. You would have been fired a long time ago if you weren't actually good at something."

Stevie's little pep talk didn't reassure me of my safety at Gisele. The only thing I was good at doing at Gisele was being Stevie's straight girlfriend.

I COULD USUALLY tell how well a meeting with Savannah would go by the behaviour of her head of snakes. They seemed disinterested when I entered her office. That was a very good indication. They were only interested if there was going to be humiliation and tears.

Savannah's facial muscles were struggling to smile from lack of use as I sat down solemnly at her desk.

"You performance has been satisfactory so this should be a quick meeting."

Indeed, there were no surprises, since Savannah was very quick at telling me when I sucked anyway. This meeting was a summary of those times. Having someone tell you how much you suck again still burned the second time around but it was like getting dumped again by a boyfriend with whom you got back together– expected and inevitable. You could see it coming and brace yourself. I almost wasn't listening.

But then Savannah completely surprised me with a raise. It was unfathomable to me that she deemed me worthy of a raise. She said it so off-hand and quickly that I almost missed it. It was only three thousand dollars and it was probably because they undercut my starting salary due to my lack of negotiation skills, but hey, I'll take whatever I could get.

"Thanks," I said, unable to hide my surprise.

A snake from Savannah's head of snakes smirked at me, no doubt smug in the knowledge of how much more Savannah made than me. Or maybe, the snake was trying to smile at me and like Savannah, a genuine smile looked strange and out-of-place. I dared to smile back at the snake.

"Keep up the good work," Savannah tried to forced a smile again. I wasn't sure what work I was good at but I was grateful to be let off so easy.

"Oh and by the way, our research budget got cut so we can't conduct the multi-mascara research you had recommended. You'll need to come up with another idea that costs nothing. Next week, please."

My mouth and heart dropped. I had spent countless hours setting it up with the research company and it was scheduled to take place next week. Most of the budget had been spent. "It's too late. I don't think I can cancel it at this point."

"I'm sure you'll find a way," Savannah answered. "Things are going so well. Don't mess it up now." *Oh, but what clever timing to break the news, you little devil.* "And I'm still waiting to hear about your innovative ideas for the Phat Lash launch."

I couldn't wait to tell Stevie that he was right. And ask him to save my ass again. I headed straight to his cube.

To my confusion and horror, Stevie was packing boxes.

"Did you get fired?" I asked, panicked. He needed to save my ass. How would my ass survive without Stevie?

"No, no, quite the opposite!" Stevie was beaming. "I got promoted to manager. I'm moving to an office!"

There was a moment of silence while I tried to absorb my reaction. Was I jealous? What would happen to our relationship now that he was my superior? How horrible a friend was I that I was not instantly happy for him but jealous?

"Congratulations!" I finally said, hoping that my face had not betrayed my evil thoughts. "Well-deserved." It was well-deserved. Stevie was the only person who made any sense at Gisele when he spoke. I tried to remember where he ranked in Chloe's Tracker.

"Thanks – we can finally speak privately in my office without my cube neighbours hearing everything." OMG, they hear *everything*? "How fa-bu is that?"

"It's definitely fa-bu," I repeated, deciding not to tell him about my measly raise. Besides, now that I knew his cube neighbours could hear *everything*, it would be inappropriate and unprofessional.

"So how did your performance review go?" Stevie asked.

"It was OK," I shrugged. "You were right. No big deal."

I WAS SURPRISED to get a text from Jamie inviting me out to a celebration dinner with Stevie that Friday night. This was the first time I would see Jamie since the barren conversation and unfortunately, I had no change in status since then, except for growing desperation. But this night was all about Stevie and how much more wonderful he was than me so hopefully the topic of barrenness wouldn't come up.

I was horrified by my jealousy and was trying to grapple with my wicked thoughts. Stevie already had it all – a great boyfriend, perfect fashion sense and a new promotion. A celebration dinner was a little *ooh, I'm so happy, in your face.* Was it not?

"Thanks for coming," Jamie hugged me when I arrived at Blowfish, Stevie's favourite sushi restaurant. Jamie was so nice that I let him get away with hugging me even though we only met once before.

"I wouldn't want to miss the big celebration dinner!" I wondered if Blowfish served Jäger?

"Oh no, please don't think of it like that. It's just an excuse for Stevie to spend time with people he loves. After all, what good is success if you can't share it with people you love?"

So true, Oprah, and way to make me feel like a small, small person for feeling jealous of such wonderful people.

"It would be pretty lonely," I agreed, my selfish thoughts banished by the mention of Oprah, the gleaming beacon of all that is good with humanity.

"You didn't tell Stevie that you were coming did you?" Jamie asked. "I want him to be surprised."

"I kept it secret because you promised not to talk about my barrenness," I said.

"Right," Jamie laughed. "You have nothing to worry about – you're young, beautiful, vivacious, you have it all." I really needed to get more gay friends. "Stevie gushes about you all the time. He just adores you. Thanks for being such a great friend to Stevie."

I smiled to cover up my guilt. Yup, feeling like an asshole right about now…

No wonder Stevie was terrified of losing Jamie. How perfect was he? Hell, I like Jamie so much, I'm terrified of Stevie losing Jamie!

"You're really wonderful to Stevie too," I continued the love fest.

"He's over the moon about you."

"Really?" Jamie asked, like a little schoolboy in love. Before I could puke from the nausea that comes from being exposed to people obnoxiously in love, I was distracted by squeals.

Stevie's other friends had arrived and the love fest unceremoniously ended. They looked and sounded identically phony and annoying except that one had man boobs, inappropriately displayed in his ill-fitting shirt. It was also evident that he was cold.

"Oh, you must be Stevie's latest fag hag," one said to me as I introduced myself, while Man Boobs giggled.

"What?" I was horrified that Stevie actually considered such tasteless ruffians to be friends. But I was also strangely redeemed, as it made me feel less small and evil. Self-reassurance was all about relativity. Find a benchmark low enough and you could possibly be Mother freakin' Theresa.

"Don't listen to them," Jamie told me as they ran off to the bar to order saké. "They're a little immature."

"The new lighting on the CN Tower is so tacky. It looks like a giant dildo," I heard Ruffian complain loudly as Jamie and I took a seat at our table.

"I don't know what kind of sex parties *you* go to, but can you please invite me next time?" Man Boobs retorted.

"Oh, honey, you're as desperate as a woman who needs a good vag-azzling." Ruffian responded nonsensically. I wisely decided against asking Jamie for a translation.

Ruffian and Man Boobs were worth it when Stevie arrived and was so touched that he seemed to fight off tears.

"Jamie's a god," Man Boobs gushed to Stevie in clear range of Jamie. "Where have you been hiding him?"

"Keep your hands off of him!" Stevie said as a mock warning.

"No chance of that! Just don't fuck it up. He's yours to lose." Terror washed over Stevie's face as my mouth dropped open in disbelief. Man Boobs was *way* nastier than Ruffian!

"Stevie, you couldn't possibly screw it up." I interjected. "Jamie's madly in love with you. Seriously, take it from a barren lady. It's *nauseating.*"

Stevie laughed and I was glad to briefly distract him from the evil forces of Ruffian and Man Boobs.

"So, how do you know Stevie?" Man Boobs turned his unwanted attention towards me.

"I work with Stevie at Gisele." I said, leaning away from him, disgusted, as if I were Heidi and he were a carb.

"Ew. How could you sell that shit?" Ruffian scowled, another unwanted participant of the conversation.

"Pardon me?"

"Cosmetics are tested on animals and cause cancer."

I was speechless as I tried to process the onslaught of nastiness. *Cancer?*

"I only wear organic makeup that hasn't been tested on animals," Man Boobs said, seeming to feed off of my visible distress. Ironically, they cared more about animal welfare than basic humanity to people.

"How do you know that's true?" I asked, uncomfortable having my values challenged by such unwholesome and unlikable people.

"Ask Stevie. When he started working at Gisele, we sent him all the information he needs to know about the issue," Ruffian smirked.

"Why don't you educate yourself about your job?" Man Boobs added smugly.

I felt sick to my stomach. I realized that the whole table was silent as Jamie and Stevie awkwardly listened to the whole exchange.

"Hey newsflash, Ronnie," Stevie came to my rescue with the one thing he knew best – fashion. "Denim on denim is back. Can you believe it?"

"Was it ever in?" Man Boobs sneered.

"Yeah, but you weren't born yet so you wouldn't know," Jamie finally shut Man Boobs down.

"Does that mean I get to drink as many espressos as I want like a civilized person again?" I asked Stevie.

"It means you can stop pretending that you're not." Stevie laughed.

Ruffian and Man Boobs were momentarily disarmed in their confusion while Jamie smiled, letting Stevie and me have our moment.

I may be Stevie's fag hag but at least I'm a fag hag who cares. So take that, you nasty ruffians.

Despite the fact that Ruffian and Man Boobs were nasty little assholes, their accusations of cancer and animal abuse had been haunting me ever since the dinner. I couldn't subdue my conscience with Stevie since he was suddenly much less accessible, pulled into the responsibilities of his new managerial role. As a result, I found myself spending a lot of quality time with Sydney. Sydney was cool but I admittedly felt less fabulous in her company.

"So your market research idea went over OK with Savannah," I was updating Sydney over espresso by the garden. The garden seemed lackluster without Stevie's glittering personality but Caden soon arrived in all his glorious manhood and my world was happy again.

"Of course," she replied.

"But the research budget got cut so I had to cancel."

"Shit. You're screwed."

"Thanks for the reassurance. Any ideas?"

As Sydney racked her brain, I watched Heidi and her entourage at the bar. Although I was not proficient at reading lips, I could see Jasmine Tit, saying "my boyfriend" several times. I gritted my teeth as I saw Chloe flirt shamelessly with Caden. Tackier than denim on denim. Her makeup looked gaudy compared to Heidi's toned down version of herself. A flash went off in my head and this time it wasn't caused by Caden's teeth.

"Never mind, I just thought of something." I said.

"What?"

"I don't need to pay mascara-obsessed women to tell me about their insecurities. They're right here in the building." I gestured towards the coffee bar.

"You're crazy if you think they're going to help you." I was crazy if I was going to share any more of my brilliant idea with Sydney. Heidi owed me and now she could finally pay me back.

"Speaking of insanity," I changed the subject. "Stevie's friends are *crazy*. Nasty little buggers. They called me a fag hag!"

Sydney laughed. "Nasty, but it's true."

"They told Stevie not to screw up his relationship with Jamie."

"They're probably just jealous." Sydney shrugged.

"Oh and get this. They got on this freaking high horse about cosmetics causing cancer and how they're tested on animals."

"Yeah, it sucks about the animal testing. I've never heard of the cancer thing. But I'd rather not think about it. Ignorance is bliss, right?"

I don't know if I ever was blissful but ever since Ruffian and Man Boobs planted the seed, I was certainly no longer ignorant. Sydney was nice in her own passive-aggressive way, but I needed Stevie.

Unfortunately, Stevie was totally AWOL and whenever I saw a glimpse of him, he seemed to have an unusually harried look about him. It was a little disturbing for me to see Stevie, the eye of my storm, to be so visibly out of sorts.

The next week, I stopped by his office one late night before I left. His office, usually impeccably organized, looked like it had morphed into a hoarder's house. He hadn't fully unpacked yet from his move so there were still half unpacked boxes, several old food containers and haphazard stacks of folders and paper piled precariously high.

"Hey, how's it going stranger?" Unable to enter his office, I leaned against at the doorway, crossing my arms.

"Good, good," he was clearly lying. "Sorry I've been so MIA. Things are super busy, I'm trying to get up to speed but there's been a product recall and one of my launches is delayed…and I don't really know what I'm doing…it's a complete nightmare."

"I understand. Are you leaving soon?"

"Yeah, yeah, I just have to finish something first. Or maybe a couple of things…"

"Maybe you should just call it a day and leave now. You can't get much done when you're tired," I suggested. I decided it was a bad time to ask him about cancer and animal abuse.

"Do I look tired?" Stevie asked, alarmed that his cover was blown.

"No," I lied. "It's late so if you're not tired you wouldn't be human. Come on, let's go."

"You're right," he sighed. He grabbed his man bag off the floor. That's when I knew something was really wrong. Ordinarily Stevie would *never* put his Louis Vuitton on the floor.

"Is everything OK?" I asked as we headed out.

"Yeah, great, why do you ask?"

"No reason, you just seemed a little distracted…"

Stevie sighed audibly again. "I can't get Irving's words out of my head."

"Who's Irving?"

"Do you remember him from the dinner at Blowfish?" Ew, that was his name? No wonder he was nasty. With a name like that, it was his destiny.

"Yeah, what's up with your friends? They're mean, horrible people."

Stevie shook his head apologetically. "They don't take well to new people but they're super fun —"

"Who cares if they're super fun if they're super douche bags? You know you deserve way better than that, right? So, what did Irving say that bothered you, other than absolutely everything?"

"He told me not to fuck it up with Jamie and it's just…totally messing with my head."

"And that's exactly why he said it – to mess with you. Don't listen to Irving. His name's *Irving*. And he has man boobs."

"I call them moobs."

"Anyway, he's just jealous. He's so insecure that he needs to make people feel bad just so he can feel better about his moobs."

"But I really am scared that I'm going to screw it up, even before Irving said anything. He just made me more paranoid about it. It's all I worry about now."

"You're so tired and overworked you're not thinking straight. You should take a cab home. I'll convince you how ridiculous you are some other time."

Stevie agreed he needed to get some sleep but I was worried. I would have never thought three months ago that I would be in this position – comforting and giving advice to my mentor at Gisele. I hoped his crisis would pass soon and I would get my Stevie back. He has a well-dressed ass to save.

Chapter 14: Enlightened

I WAS COUNTING DOWN TO The Enlightened's show at The Rivoli like it was 1999. Leading up to Carpenter Boy's gig, I sent countless texts, emails and Facebook messages until Jackie told me she wouldn't go if she received one more f'ing reminder. Calista asked me if I was going to set up a Facebook Fan Page for the event because if so, she would sabotage it. Lindsay told me I was obsessing about the event more than she was obsessing about her wedding and it was not normal.

Stevie was still swept up with the Perfect Storm of his new assignment. He hadn't responded to my stalker texts. I hoped that he wasn't ignoring me. It wasn't the show that I cared about so much, it was the fact that Stevie and my girls were finally going to meet. I may have been a little obsessively nervous that they wouldn't get along. The Merging of the Friends was sometimes an awkward and disappointing affair.

My girls showed up promptly on time and were justifiably annoyed when I showed up half an hour late, unable to steal away from work any earlier. I apologized profusely and thanked them excessively.

"Stop being so desperate," Jackie advised. "It's irritating."

"So where's the amazing Stevie?" Lindsay asked.

"Oh, he must be running late from work," I covered up for him. I had run by his office to pick him up, but he wasn't there, despite the fact that I had sent several emails and texts. I was running so late that instead of trying to track him down I texted him in the cab.

"This place is cool," Calista said. "I like it so much better than those phony chi-chi bars around your work."

"You don't like those places? Why didn't you say so before?"

Calista shrugged. "It's easier for you."

"I hope this place isn't too underground for Stevie," I looked around worriedly. It wasn't really Stevie's scene.

"Well, given that it isn't actually an underground bar," Jackie said. "I think you're good."

"Why are you obsessing about Stevie like he's your boyfriend?" Lindsay asked.

"I'm not obsessing about him, I'm just worried because he's excessively hygienic. Dirty places freak him out a little," I defended Stevie.

"This is a bar in downtown Toronto, not Calcutta," Calista said. "So unless he's OCD, I wouldn't worry about it."

"He may be a little OCD, but not in the clinical sense," I said.

"He sounds like a blast," Lindsay said. "Where is he? The show's about to start any minute."

"Um…" I checked my cell phone for text messages. There it was – a cancellation text.

```
So sorry gorgeousness, work emergency. Can't make
it tonight.
```

I was disappointed and embarrassed. Stevie never let me down and now he was doing it in front of my girls.

"Something came up at work and he can't make it," I tried to brush it off casually. "That sucks."

"Wow, he just pulled a Veronica," Jackie said. Calista and Lindsay laughed in agreement.

I was horrified. Was this how I made them feel every time I cancelled? "Is that an actual term you guys use?"

"Well it's true," Lindsay said. "You can't be offended by the truth."

"He just got promoted and is having a really tough time at work. He's working crazy hours," I decided to defend Stevie rather than myself.

"Sounds familiar," Lindsay said.

"Anyway, it's only temporary. He better snap out of it. I need him around to save my ass at work!" I tried to make light of it but could tell that my girls were not impressed by Stevie.

"Never mind your ass, who's going to save your soul?" Calista asked.

I thought that was a bizarre comment but wasn't able to ask since Carpenter Boy's band came on. I was expecting a painful hour of loud incomprehensible punk rock but they were surprisingly quite good. It was a catchy combination of funk, punk and pop. I was digging them. I pointed out Carpenter Boy to my girls. They nodded and smiled in approval. Nothing like lead singer status to turn an average looking boy attractive. Come to think of it, the audience was overwhelmingly female. Still dressed in my trendy, try-to-impress-Caden, over-priced outfit from work, I realized I stuck out like a sore thumb from the casual, under-stated style of rest of the crowd.

Then I recognized the drummer. It was Naked Towel Boy. Yay! Mystery solved. Or at least part-way solved. What was the drummer doing alone in Carpenter Boy's condo taking a shower?

"The drummer! He's Naked Towel Boy!" I yelled to Jackie.

"He's hot!"

"Gay?"

She squinted her eyes in concentration and then shook her head. "I hope not. You can have the lead singer. Drummer boy's mine."

That was a good sign. Jackie generally wasn't attracted to homosexuals. She would undoubtedly hit on Naked Towel Boy and solve the ambiguous, sexual preference mystery.

After the show, the band was surrounded by female fans. Feeling out of place, I suddenly felt reluctant to go speak to Carpenter Boy. Calista, Lindsay and Jackie prodded and pushed me to go congratulate him as aggressively and irritatingly as toddler beauty pageant moms.

"Come on," Jackie shoved me in the direction of the stage.

"OK, OK, quit it," I yelled and nearly bumped into Carpenter Boy as he approached.

"Hi!" My girls and I chimed in unison, smiling and standing at attention.

"Hey, Veronica, you made it! I'm flattered."

"Great show! These are my friends," I introduced them, praying that they would remain cool and subtle. It soon became painfully obvious from the ensuing interrogation that I had brought my girl friends to check him out.

"Your *girlfriend* must think your band's so cool!" Lindsay said. I could feel my face growing red.

He laughed good-naturedly. "Uh no, don't really have a girlfriend." I was laser focused between his eyes and Jackie's boobs to see whether he was checking out her boobs.

"Really? You must have your pick of girls!" That was Calista's not-so-subtle observation. I shook my head, willing them to please stop with my eyes. My face was starting to burn with embarrassment.

"Uh, not really. They're really all here for the drummer. Chicks dig him." Indeed, Naked Towel Boy appeared to be in his natural habitat, now shirtless and swarmed by chicks.

"But does he dig chicks?" Jackie jumped in. "I mean, are you sure he's not gay?"

"Gay?" He laughed. "I've never heard a girl ask that question. He's definitely very heterosexual."

"Are you gay?" Jackie asked. I cringed and actually covered my eyes with my hand.

"Uh…" he looked confused. "No…"

"Good, let's all go hit on the drummer," Jackie suggested and dragged Calista and Lindsay with her, leaving Will and I standing alone in the awkward aftermath of the assault.

"Wow, your friends are really, uh, forward."

"Yeah…sorry about that," I apologized. "You took it pretty well."

He nodded and shrugged. "How's the Ikea unit?"

"The…? Oh, yeah, it's back in the box."

He laughed. "Well, the offer still stands…I mean, for me to come over and help assemble it."

"I don't think you're gay," I blurted. He looked confused and unfortunately a little offended. "I saw the naked drummer taking a shower alone in your condo." I tried to explain.

"What?" He looked startled.

"No! I mean, I, uh, knocked on your door and he answered it in a towel."

"Oh," he said, relieved. "Lucky you."

"I have a gay boyfriend so I guess I just think everyone's gay now."

"Your boyfriend's gay?" His face betrayed his disappointment.

"No! I don't have a boyfriend. It's my friend. Totally platonic. He's gay and I call him my gay boyfriend…'cause it's…it's funny."

Will's face showed confusion and complete lack of agreement that it was funny. "I don't get it," he said.

This was possibly more awkward than my conversations with Caden. It clearly wasn't working out and I needed to end the pain immediately. "OK, well, I guess I'll see you around." And I bolted.

Perhaps the painful experience with Carpenter Boy would prepare me for the painful snake lashing when I presented my free research plan to Savannah.

I knocked hesitantly on her open door. "Savannah, do you have a moment? I have a solution to the Phat Lash research."

She nodded. "Make it fast."

"I have a crazy idea," I said as I tentatively entered her evil lair.

Savannah made an expression as if she were constipated. Probably not the best opening line.

"What if we just have a focus group with Gisele employees?" I continued, trying to sound confident. "We would give them free Phat Lash before it hits the market and an invitation to the Gi-Spot party. Stevie could be the moderator – every girl feels safe confiding to a gay guy."

There was an agonizingly long silence as I braced myself for the impact of her scathing response. Her Medusa head of snakes were strangely silent.

"Well, what the hell are you waiting for? Go, go – do it!" She ushered me out of her office with her hands.

I stood in shock for a moment. Had I actually escaped the inevitable snake lashing and gained Savannah's approval?

"Go!" She practically yelled. "Before I change my mind."

I smiled and all but ran out of her office. "Thanks!"

Stevie was virtually impossible to find and so it was my good fortune that I ran into him on my way back to my cube. I was happy to give him the good news in person.

"Stevie, about last night, you suck!"

"I'm delighted that you're so happy about it," Stevie replied.

"And Savannah has approved of how you're going to make up for it!" Stevie looked alarmed. "You're going to moderate a focus group of Gisele employees for me! Yay, Stevie saves the day! Again!"

Stevie's face blanched. He did not look nearly as excited as I thought he would. "When?" he asked nervously. "It's kinda crazy this week…"

"Oh, come on! It'll be fun!" I jokingly punched him in the arm. He recoiled.

"Ow!" he exclaimed, rubbing his arm.

"Sorry, I guess I underestimated my own strength," I laughed. "Or you're gayer than I thought."

"Well, I guess I don't really have a choice if you already spoke to Savannah," he said.

"Oh sorry," I realized that perhaps it was a little presumptuous of me to volunteer Stevie without first asking him. "I should have asked you first but I thought you'd love the idea. Isn't it a great idea?"

"Super," he replied and walked away.

A wave of guilt passed over me for a moment. I convinced myself that he was distracted or late for a meeting and the wave of guilt was soon gone.

It was easy to cancel the project with the research company without penalty when I subtly suggested they would face the wrath of Savannah otherwise. Also, it was a shame that this project got cancelled but we had so many more exciting research projects coming up. Having worked with Savannah before, they insisted the work performed thus far be *pro bono* because they loved working with Gisele and please do consider them for the upcoming research projects.

I would remember the weight that comes with dropping the Savannah bomb. Quite conveniently, the research company had already emailed me the discussion guides which I happily passed on to Stevie.

Next step: focus group participants. Easy. Heidi owed me and she was the queen bee of Gisele, as I had shamelessly addressed her when I asked for the favour. She happily recruited two dozen of insecure mascara-obsessed colleagues, or as I had graciously described, fashion-forward, trend-setting cosmetic connoisseurs who believed the most important accessory to any outfit was mascara.

Despite my ingenuity and brilliance, it was gnawing at me that Stevie hadn't asked me yet how my encounter with Carpenter Boy had gone, nor did he seem excited to help me with the focus groups. He was a poor version of himself, like a bad Louis Vuitton knock-off. I had proven that I could get by now without his help but Gisele was a lot less fun without him. I'd rather stumble with Stevie than get by on my own.

Just when my guilt was subsiding, Stevie asked me to text Jamie and explain why Stevie was canceling another date night. He also asked me to add that I was fully to blame. Slightly concerned for his emotional stability, I went along with it as if it weren't a desperate plea. I hoped that he would bring his fabulous fierceness to my focus groups.

The night of the focus groups, I had flowers delivered to Stevie's office as thanks and in the hopes of lightening his mood.

I set up a conspicuous video camera to record the sessions, knowing that Stevie and Heidi's mean girls would cooperate if conscious that they were being recorded. Stevie arrived and surprisingly appeared to be in very good spirits. I hoped that his good spirits hadn't been influenced by drinking spirits. I needed him to be sober.

"My manager is super impressed that I'm leading these groups," Stevie said to me as I decorated the room with various mascara products and advertising examples. "Apparently your idea has caught the attention of senior management and it's considered very innovative. Thanks for including me!"

I wasn't surprised that Savannah hadn't shared this praise with me but was surprised that Stevie was only eager to help now that he knew he would directly benefit.

Heidi and her mean girls started to arrive. Heidi may have been the queen bee of Gisele but that did not mean that everyone adored her like Chloe and Jasmine. Also keenly aware of the senior management interest in this research initiative, Heidi had obediently recruited the profile I had requested, even if they despised her and her entourage. Heidi's excessive hair and makeup had returned in full force.

"Ladies, looking fierce tonight!" Stevie kissed them on the cheek as they entered the room. "Are those new boobs? Fab, girl!" Stevie was working the mean girls like the mayor of hot girl-ville. I had not anticipated the profound impact of gathering a group of insecure, shallow twenty-something year old hot girls in one room. The air was thick with perfume, insecurity and contempt.

"Snap," Chloe said in approval of Heidi's high end escort look as she took a seat beside her.

Holly, the Queen Bee of Bitchy Clique #2, was decidedly not in agreement with Chloe and scoffed from across the table. "Hey, Chloe; 2005 called. They want their line back."

Chloe scowled at her. Holly's standings in the Chloe Tracker had no doubt plummeted down to the bottom of the list. "Shut up, you skinny bitch."

Holly perfectly lined lips smiled nastily. "Thanks. I didn't know you thought I was skinny."

"This is *awesome*," I gushed to Stevie.

Before Chloe could lunge across the table at Holly, Stevie loudly and jovially announced that he would be turning on the camera.

"Now now, girls, smile and look pretty for the camera," he advised, hands on hips. Chloe grudgingly settled into her seat, shooting daggers at Holly.

"You need to leave now," he told me as he fiddled with the camera.

"What? I can't stay? This is my research," I insisted, outraged.

"I want my ladies to be comfortable confiding in me without feeling scrutinized." Stevie smiled lovingly at his ladies of the night.

"They're being recorded," I pointed out.

"I want her to leave too," Chloe piped up. The room unanimously agreed. At least they agreed on one thing.

I pretended to graciously comply, hoping that Stevie was merely buttering up his ladies of the night and not favouring a room full of hot insecure girls to his fabulous Ronnie.

Chapter 15: Self-Proclaimed Hot Girl

I DON'T KNOW WHY I had doubted Stevie's loyalty towards me or his brilliance in manipulating hot girls. Stevie was back on top of my world with his usual fabulousness. We watched the DVDs together in awe and admiration of both his artistry and the confessions of these self-proclaimed hot girls. He was masterful at encouraging them to share their genius with the world of less fortunate-looking people.

It was a curious exposé into the psyche of a self-proclaimed hot girl. Much like SUVs feel they are entitled to more of the road than their smaller counterparts, so hot girls feel they are entitled to more out of life than their less hot counterparts. Indeed, hot girls should never wait in line at a club or restaurant; should always get first dibs; should never have to get out of the way for anyone, including vehicles; and God forbid, should never be told that something is sold out or fully booked. But with self-proclaimed hotness and all the associated benefits of such entitlement comes the price of maintaining the esteemed title of hot girl. It was astounding that such hotness could drive so much desperate insecurity of losing said hotness.

The other oddity that struck me was their crippling obsession of the male opinion. I thought it was only Jasmine Tit who could not exist without the approval of her boyfriend but it became very clear that all self-proclaimed hot girls live in constant fear of lack of approval of their future boyfriends.

Mascara was the one cosmetic must-have that these self-proclaimed hot girls felt had the most significant contribution to their hotness. They believed that they were unrecognizable without mascara. They wouldn't be caught ugly without it.

Based on these confessions, Stevie and I formulated our recommendations for repositioning Gisele's mascara portfolio to drive multi-mascara usage: Emergency Mascara (a smaller mascara wand that would fit in a small clutch); Night Out Mascara (a dramatic mascara for social nighttime occasions); Everyday Mascara (a less ostentatious but effective mascara for everyday use); and Diva Mascara (false eyelashes plus mascara combo kit for special occasions). Within each of these mascara usage occasions we proposed different benefits, like lengthening, thickening, and colour.

And thanks to Stevie's masterful facilitation, I was able to unearth from the DVD confessions an innovative marketing idea to launch Phat Lash. I learned that being the hottest girl in the room can be stressful to maintain. People look up to them for always being on the cutting edge of fashion and beauty. It's an important role they play for those less fortunate-looking. But sometimes it's hard to keep up with all the trends when hot girls have such enviably cool on-the-go lifestyles. Enter: Hot girl brand ambassadors. Cosmetic companies send hot girl brand ambassadors free products and if they love it, they talk and blog about it. And because so many people look up to hot girls, what hot girls love instantly becomes a big hit when the less fortunate-looking copy them in the hopes that they could be just a fraction as hot as them. Supposedly. Savannah no doubt was a self-proclaimed hot girl so her approval of my hot girl brand ambassador idea would be the ultimate litmus test.

In the meantime, now that the agencies were briefed, everything was going swimmingly well with the Gi-Spot party planning. The fruits of my labour would finally be revealed in a big meeting I had booked with Caden in which the agencies would present the final event proposal. The account managers were all women and were tripping over themselves to impress Caden. *Get in line, beeyatches, get in line.* The beeyatches were assembling an invite list of local celebrities and socialites and securing MTV and Fashion Television to cover the event. Based on viewing the racy UK Gi-Spot TV ad, they were recommending an edgy S&M-inspired theme (sushi and martini) for the party.

The event planners would love for it to take place in Berkely Church because there was something very naughty about the juxtaposition of a sinful S&M party in a church. Throughout the venue would be various "sin" themes carried out, each representing one of the Seven Deadly Sins: Gluttony would be the bar; Vanity would be the make-up stations; Wrath would be the dominatrix bartenders and waitresses; Envy would be the runway fashion show; Lust would be the topless male models serving martinis and sushi; Greed would be the generous swag bags; and Sloth would be the massage stations. I knew Caden would love it.

As the successful party planning progressed, so did Caden's approval of me. I had come up with the idea to have a "Where is the Gi-Spot?" teaser campaign directed at local media, socialites, celebrities and Gisele. Greatly amused at how naughty I was, Caden had given the go-ahead to send the invitations out immediately. It was thrilling to get Caden's encouraging emails and supportive smiles at the coffee bar. It was obvious that he was flirting with me. Sydney refused to give the topic the time of day but if Stevie were around, I was sure he'd agree. And I didn't have to get a boob job or dress like a high end escort!

"How's Britney?" I dared to ask Caden at the coffee bar one day.

"Great girl, but we're not together any more," he smiled.

"That's too bad," I said, wildly celebrating inwardly. Sydney yanked my arm disapprovingly as I blushed and smiled shyly.

Feeling particularly daring and confident one day in my sexy librarian garb, I stopped by Caden's office to deliver non-critical news of additional editorial coverage I secured for the Gi-Spot launch. The door was closed. I hesitated to knock and decided against it.

Just as I was turning away, the door opened to reveal Chloe. Suddenly and unwittingly face to face, we glowered momentarily at one another and stopped only when Caden came up behind Chloe and greeted me like a long lost friend, or as I liked to think, lover.

"Veronica! To what do I owe the pleasure of your visit?"

Chloe remained trapped between us and I was only too happy to force her to listen to my good news and ensuing praise.

"I have some great news that I wanted to share with you! The beauty editors hadn't yet received the Gi-Spot products but no worries – I called my US counterparts and had the products shipped overnight. I just got word that Gi-Spot will receive coverage in the next issue of Fashion, Flare and Elle Canada!"

Chloe's face had gone from glowering to white. She looked like she wanted to bolt for the hills and drag me behind her by the hair.

Caden looked confused. "That's strange. Chloe had confirmed that coverage weeks ago. Are you sure it's for Gi-Spot?"

Chloe remained silent and tense, glaring at me.

"Yeah, it was a huge crisis this week when the agency realized the products hadn't been sent so I got pulled in to help out," I replied. I saw Chloe's bitter, shamed expression and it suddenly hit me what had happened. Chloe had forgotten to send the products and had lied to Caden when she confirmed the editorial coverage. Despite my keen dislike for Chloe, I was mortified. It was not my style to throw my colleagues under the bus.

"I'm sorry, I didn't know…" I said with genuine apology to Chloe. Her eyes burned like a vampire's as she pushed past me.

I was truly horrified as I was left standing uncomfortably in front of Caden.

"Thanks Veronica. Anything else?" he asked, gracious in his attempt to cover up my humiliation.

I shook my head. "I think you're going to love the presentation tomorrow."

"With you in charge, I know I will," he replied softly.

With all my work drama, I was unable to help out with the party planning for Calista's congratulations party. Now I knew how annoying I was when I was planning our outing to see Carpenter Boy's band. Maybe my girls had just put it off until the last minute or maybe they were closet party planning monsters, relentlessly contacting me for input and ideas. One would have thought this was Calista's Sweet 16 party on MTV. Calista would have been just as happy if her closest friends got together at our favourite pub. I knew they thought I was blowing them off by replying I was good with whatever they decided and to go ahead planning without me. But didn't they know I was busy during the week? I just wanted them to tell me what to bring.

Lindsay was particularly disappointed that I didn't want to ask Carpenter Boy's band to play at Calista's party. Maybe I would have humiliated myself again if it were U2, but I saw through it as Lindsay's last feeble attempt to try and set me up with her carpenter fantasy.

The bash was held Saturday night in the party room of Jackie's downtown condo. It was certainly festively decorated, although I was surprised that a few decorations had consumed so much time. When I saw the spread of food, I realized that Lindsay prepared many of the hors d'oeuvres herself. For the first time, I felt a slight pang of guilt that my job prevented me from helping out. However, with Jackie in charge of alcohol tonight, my girls would shortly forgive me. There was a DJ setting up, probably one of Jackie's "friends".

I arrived late because I had been working all day and had dedicated a considerable amount of timing preparing myself to look fabulous to wow the friends I hadn't seen in awhile with my glamourous new job and exciting lifestyle. Apparently all the preparation was for nought. Perhaps I was out of touch with my friends longer than I thought but I didn't recognize anyone. I walked through the sparse groups of people, trying to pick out a familiar face.

"Am I just old and prudish, or are Lady Gaga's videos disturbing?" I heard one person ask.

"No, you're not old, just a prude," her friend confirmed.

"Who are these people?" I asked Jackie. I found her in the first placed I looked, making drinks at the bar.

"They're Calista's friends from her PhD program. Interesting crowd." she responded diplomatically as she made me a gin and tonic.

"Drink up," she winked as she slid the tumbler across the bar towards me.

I coughed when I realized I was drinking straight gin. "Did you put any tonic in this?"

"You're late. You need to catch up." And with that she poured us shots.

"Where's the fashion show?" Lindsay asked as she approached us. The question was directed at my outfit and if I wasn't mistaken, may have had as heavy a dose of sarcasm as the gin in my drink. Perhaps I was a little over dressed in my flouncy, strapless mini-dress and platform pumps, I speculated as I surveyed the crowd. Economists dress really boring.

"Thanks," I responded. "Hey Jackie, Lindsay missed the shots, another round of shots for the ladies!"

"Uh, maybe you should have a glass of water instead," Lindsay said, looking at my two empty glasses consumed in just the first few minutes of my arrival. "Have you had a chance to eat dinner? Maybe you should fill up on hors d'oeuvres. By the way, you paid for all the food."

"Yeah dude, this isn't a frosh party," Jackie said as she poured us shots. "Have a little class."

I smiled approvingly at Jackie's "classy" shots. I'm going to need a few drinks to stomach this crowd.

"Are you still pissed off about Carpenter Boy?" I asked Lindsay.

"No, I'm disappointed again that you always put your stupid job ahead of your best friends," Lindsay answered.

"Wow, that's a harsh statement," I said. "And completely unfair."

"Ladies, let's not argue on Calista's special night," Jackie interrupted. "Speaking of which, the party girl's coming. Another round of shots for Calista!"

The crowd started to pick up, or maybe it was the multiple other shots that made it more palatable. I don't remember who I met but I do remember that I definitely have the coolest job. I also vaguely recall Lindsay trying to silence me physically a number of times. I may have been yelling to people about my Gi-Spot and introducing myself as a professional sex party planner. I'm pretty sure Jackie called me a cab and let Lindsay drag me out of the party when I started yelling that I was at the top of The Tracker and harassing the men into declaring that I was the hottest girl at the party.

I was severely hung over the morning after. Embarrassing remnants of the night passed over me like nausea. I don't know what made me want to puke more – the hangover or the embarrassment. I dragged my sorry disheveled ass out of bed at noon to buy Pepto Bismol and Gatorade from the corner store. I was unshowered, wearing dirty jeans and a ratty T-shirt, my hair in a sloppy ponytail.

"Hung over?" the cashier asked me when he saw my purchases.

No shit.

"No." Bitter in my hungover state, I didn't want to grant the inappropriate cashier the benefit of being right.

And of course, the karmic gods were pissing their pants laughing as I ran into Carpenter Boy in the elevator, hugging my hangover remedies close to my chest, trying not to shake from the exertion of standing up vertically. I couldn't remember the last time I looked or felt this revolting. Luckily I had managed to avoid him until now, thanks to my obscure schedule. But what better time to bump into him than when we were in a closed space. All the better to smell the stench of last night's alcohol leaking from my pores.

"Rough night?" he asked.

"Uh…yeah," I replied head down, leaning against the elevator wall, praying that I would make it to my condo without puking.

"You know what the best hangover remedy is?" he asked. I forced myself to lift my head and look up at him pathetically. "A beer!"

I winced.

"Just kidding, bad joke. Seriously, a banana milk shake with a little honey. Best remedy."

"Banana milkshake?" Just saying those words made me want to projectile hurl. "That's disgusting." Almost as disgusting as me right now. This elevator ride was taking *forever*.

"It works – I swear."

"I would puke. But thanks." The elevator doors finally opened and I bolted as quickly as my incapacitated body would allow me.

"Wanna borrow some bananas? Last call," he asked as he kept pace with my slow, pained hobble. I couldn't tell whether he was mocking me.

I shook my head and barely made it into my condo before I dry-heaved glamourously into the bathroom sink. I was not a hot girl right now.

There were a couple of text messages on my phone that morning. One was from Lindsay that said "WTF?" and another one from Jackie asking me what the hell my obsession with hot girls was. Her follow-up message was "btw: so not hot." Nothing from Calista.

The rest of the day was a total write off. I was planning on spending Sunday at the office trying to get caught up on work but instead spent the day hydrating myself and miserably hoping the hangover would pass. But alas, it was a full day punishment. Nor did the shame pass. I couldn't bring myself to apologize to Calista that day. I thought a text would be tacky and talking was still as painful as thinking about a banana milkshake. Calista called in the evening but I convinced myself that it was OK not to answer. She would understand. After I make up big time for my childish and selfish behaviour. I was awful – I didn't even remember congratulating her that night. Come to think of it, I may have bitched to her about cancer and animal abuse for awhile. She didn't leave a message.

When I was able to sit upright in bed without feeling nauseous, I googled hangover remedies. Hey, what do you know banana milk-shake with honey was right up there. Carpenter Boy wasn't f'ing with me after all. I googled friend remedies, thinking that I might need it soon. Despite the hundreds of suggestions for hangover remedies, oddly enough there was nothing specifically dedicated to friend remedies. This one I'd have to figure out on my own.

Chapter 16: Naughty Girl

The event planning agency did a spectacular job at presenting the event and bringing the sinful themes to life with a multi-media extravaganza. They had dressed up in S&M outfits and tripped over one another to seduce Caden. Sure enough, Caden was delighted with everything, calling me his favourite naughty girl, much to the chagrin of the S&M-garbed event planners. I could tell from the envy in their eyes that they wanted to whip me with their black patent leather whips.

"It's all yours," he said to me. I saw the event planners purse their scarlet-stained lips. Their shiny patent leather outfits squeaked as they shifted with displeasure.

"I have to give full credit to the agency for their hard work and creativity." I said. I did not want to compromise my relationship with them. One Chloe in my life was all I could deal with.

"Absolutely, you've all done a tremendous job. I couldn't be happier," Caden flashed a smile at the S&M ladies and they swooned as much as their stiff leather cat suits would allow. "What I meant was the Gi-Spot product launch. Veronica, it's all yours."

"But…hasn't Chloe been working on the launch for the last year? I hate to take it from her now when it's practically done." I can just imagine what hell I would get from Chloe now that I've fully stolen her Gi-Spot from her.

"Ah, there's been a few bumps in the road and you're just the person to smooth it out. Chloe has moved on to her next project.

Besides, it would be nice to see more of you," he winked, sealing the deal.

"OK," I gushed, before realizing that I had just signed up for an unreasonable shitload more work and the wrath of Chloe.

I hoped that Caden had cleared his abundant use of my time and energy with Savannah. I knew the news that she wasn't the centre of my universe wouldn't go over well with her. Perhaps I could quell her wrath with my brilliant marketing idea. I usually never approached Savannah unless I've cleared it with her admin and confirmed that she was in a relatively non-abusive mood. However, on a whim, I decided to stop by Savanna's office unannounced. I was still on a high from Caden's approval of my naughtiness and desire to see more of it. I might as well continue the momentum.

I was standing outside Savannah's office, silently psyching myself up when I heard a strange and unusual sound coming from inside her office. Usually the sound of crying was preceded by Savannah's wild shrieks. However, the office was eerily quiet except for the sound of weeping. Before I could stop myself, I peered around the doorway to confirm the impossible. Did Savannah actually have feelings other than anger, boredom and disdain?

"Are you OK?" I asked, surprised by how genuinely concerned I sounded.

"Gucci is sick," she blurted as she delicately dabbed at her red, swollen eyes with a tissue. It looked like she had been crying for awhile.

"Oh! I'm sorry, I didn't know you were that close with the designer."

"No, no, Gucci's my dog," she gestured, tears running down her face, at a framed photo beside her computer of a pomeranian in a fluffy sweater and diamond collar. "Little G," she added with a whimper.

"He's so cute! I hope he's going to be OK."

"She." Savannah corrected. Of course, a bitch would have a bitch as a pet.

"I don't know what's wrong," she continued. "Gucci's barely eating and has no energy. I've been monitoring her behaviour and tracking it in several charts." She showed me several line and bar graphs indicating Gucci's water and food consumption and sleep patterns on an hourly basis. "My vet told me to relax and just wait and see. Is he *crazy*? I can't relax!"

"I'm sure she's fine but why don't you get a second opinion? It might make you feel better. My parents have a great vet that does house calls." My parents are alarmingly obsessed with their miniature poodle and had rejected countless vets before entrusting their current vet with the health of their baby. I knew that Savannah would expect nothing less than the obsessive-compulsive choice of my parents.

Savannah looked perplexed that she had not thought of the obvious. "Well, I'm desperate so I guess I could try that. Can you please leave? I'm having a little bit of a private moment."

As I gingerly excused myself, I noticed that the Medusa snakes were gone.

I HAD BEEN deeply dreading my transition meeting with Chloe and almost considered passing on it but Caden had arranged the meeting to ensure that all necessary transitions would happen. In fact, strangely enough, he had the meeting with the three of us in his office, as if he knew that he would need to arbitrate.

We were seated silently outside his office, waiting for his previous meeting to end. I could feel the hostility emanating from Chloe. As nasty a person as she was, it still deeply bothered me that she hated me.

"I'm sorry," I finally ventured to say. "I didn't ask for this. If it makes you feel any better, I'm not going to have a life or very much sleep until this launches."

"Whatever," she replied, looking stonily ahead. "Too bad you can't run to Stevie to solve all your problems. Are you sad that he's crashing and burning? I give him two weeks before he's fired."

"Stevie's *not* crashing and burning," I protested in fierce defense.

Chloe made a face to indicate she was in complete disagreement with my statement.

"I know you're mad at me, but please don't take this out on Stevie," I said.

"You're taking everything away from me. And now you think that you can take Caden."

I felt my chest burn. "Caden's not yours. He's your boss."

"I don't even know why I'm here if he thinks you're so perfect. You can figure it out without my transition." And with that, Chloe got up and walked away. I sat surprised and confused for a few moments until Caden opened his door.

"Where's Chloe?" he asked.

"She was here and then… she just walked away," I answered.

"Veronica, love, I'm so sorry but I just got pulled in to meetings for the rest of the day. I know you can handle it on your own. I'll talk to Chloe and make sure she hands off everything to you."

"OK," I said, shell-shocked. I had gone from Caden supplying full reinforcements to no support.

"Thank you. You're a doll," he smiled and shut his door.

Looking through Chloe's documents and emails, it became clear why she did not want to sit through a humiliating meeting with Caden and me. The timing of the launch was clearly compromised and there was no doubt that Chloe played a large part in screwing things up. She had not gotten the forecast in early enough to secure quantities at the US plant. The US had already launched and due to their wild success, were already out of stock, further putting our quantities at risk. The print creative had also been delayed because

Chloe had not passed it by legal counsel and they were now uncomfortable with the ambiguous nature of the ad, claiming that people might misconstrue that it's for their actual G-spot which may lead to improper use of the product. All in all, it was a mess.

I was nothing short of pulling out my hair and clawing out my eyes as I discovered one fire after another when Savannah stopped by my cube. She was sans Medusa head of snakes.

"How's Gucci?" I asked.

"Gucci's fine," her expression remained stern.

"Oh, good. Did you call my parent's vet?" I dared to ask.

"Yes, he was fairly competent." I waited for her to continue but she didn't.

"Well, enough about that," she broke the awkward silence. I was relieved that my parent's vet hadn't inadvertently killed Gucci but I supposed that was the last I would ever hear of her pet.

"I was surprised by your Hot Girl Brand Ambassador proposal." Savannah said.

"Oh?" I asked, holding my breath.

"Pleasantly," she continued. "It's not as horrible as I expected."

I braced myself for her the onslaught of insulting feedback but instead she said crisply, "Approved."

I wasn't sure if I had heard wrong and blinked, stunned and bewildered.

"The state of your desk is unacceptable," Savannah stated, observing the unusual disheveled nature of my desk.

Uh-oh. Here goes. "Chloe's been pulled off the Gi-Spot launch so Caden gave it all to me. There are a lot of issues with it…so… yeah…"

"What!?" Savannah practically shrieked. I flinched, waiting for the inevitable beating. "What is he trying to do? Work you to death? I'm going to have a word with him!"

My mouth dropped open in shock as Savannah strode purposely in the direction of Caden's office. Well, if the way to a bitch's heart was through her bitch, maybe I should become better friends with Heidi and Jasmine to get on Chloe's better side.

Savannah returned to my cube not more than five minutes later with a face that bore the look of compromise. "It would be good for your profile to keep the Gi-Spot launch. Caden has much praise for you —"

"He does?" I couldn't help but interrupt enthusiastically.

Savannah paused and looked at me strangely. "Yes…about your work."

"Really?" My school-girl infatuation continue to bubble from me like a just-popped bottle of champagne.

Savannah was now looking at me sternly. "Yes. I'm pleased that you are consistently competent."

"What else did he say?" I rested my chin in my hand.

"I don't know Veronica, would you like me to pass you a note at recess?" Savannah's tone had fully assumed its familiar condescension.

I clammed up and shrunk back in my chair, humiliated.

"I thought that a fair compromise would be to get you some help," she said, her voice losing a little of its edge. "Someone that you get along with." I perked up. Maybe she got Stevie to help me! "So Sydney will be assisting you on the Gi-Spot launch."

Noooooo!

"I'm sorry," I said as Sydney appeared moments later at my cube, unimpressed. It wasn't an apology to her. I really was sorry for myself that the one free hall pass I had gotten from Savannah was a wasted freebie. Sydney had the best work life balance of all Assistant Brand Managers and her reputation was such that she was very protective of it. "It's a shit show."

"I'd say," Sydney was oddly composed. "Let's see the damage."

"Sydney, Chloe said an awful thing about Stevie. Is Stevie crashing and burning?"

As Sydney paused in her deliberation, I heard a resounding *yes* through the cube walls. It was the first word that my cube neighbour, a financial planner, had ever uttered to me. I had never heard him talk before and had assumed he didn't speak English. He was a slight, very shy Asian man and so silent he seemed lifeless, a financial-bot. Most of the time I felt like the cube beside me was empty. Sydney and I looked at each other incredulously and promptly got up on my chairs to check it out.

"Excuse me," I said politely, as Sydney and I peered over the cube. "Were you speaking to us?"

He looked up at us slowly. "Yes. Stevie's in trouble. You have to help him before he gets fired."

"We've tried but he refuses our help," Sydney answered, to my surprise. I wasn't aware that she had also tried to help Stevie.

"What should we do?" I asked him. We were so desperate that I was now seeking advice from someone that I didn't think even think was alive five minutes ago.

"How the hell would I know? I'm just here to crunch numbers all day," he responded. "But could I ask you a favour? Could you please, for the love of God, stop obsessing over Caden? It's *painful* to listen to."

"Oh, ah, sorry about that." We hastily got off our chairs.

"Does everyone know about my crush?" I whispered to Sydney.

"Yes," he answered through the cube walls.

Shit, I worded back to Sydney.

"I told you," she answered. "OK, let's get this shit over with. What Chloe fuck-ups do we need to fix?" She sat down and crossed her arms.

"Are you really going to help me?" I asked in disbelief.

"Of course, and the faster we do it the faster we can help Stevie."

"You go, girl!" We heard my cube neighbour voice again. Sydney and I made disgusted faces at each other. Great that my financial-bot cube neighbour finally found his voice but did he not know cube etiquette? It also appeared that he was coming out of the closet. This could get messy.

Sydney asked that I explain each problem to her in minute detail. I was impressed with her quick resolution of the issues and decisive division of labour.

"You're good," I said, unable to hold back my surprise. "We make a good team."

"Of course, did you ever doubt me?"

"Uh…kind of," I admitted before my apparently all-knowing cube neighbour could pipe up. Beware the silent ones. Maybe they weren't so silent for their shyness but for their keen observation.

"Just because I work decent hours doesn't mean I don't work. It just means that I work very efficiently. And I'm OK if something isn't 100%. Nothing's ever going to be perfect."

"Right," I answered. Unless it's for Caden. Then it must be as perfect as him.

"Look," Sydney lowered her voice. "My oldest sister was a stock broker. She made it to VP in ten years but worked insane hours. She didn't have a life – she was lonely and sad and constantly stressed. Eventually, she had a nervous breakdown. It was really hard on the family. Now she's a struggling actress/waitress in L.A. and she's never been happier – or healthier. Life's too short. It's just a job. We're not saving babies." Sydney shrugged.

"That's beautiful," we heard my cube neighbour say. "And we all thought you were lazy."

"That's enough," I said, adding more sternness than necessary to my voice so my irritation would permeate through the cube walls.

"Thanks for sharing that," I returned my attention to Sydney. "I get why you act the way you do now and I'm sorry if I judged you. You're right – we're just selling mascara, not saving babies. Now hopefully we can convince Stevie of that."

"Yeah! Go save your baby," the now ubiquitous voice of my cube neighbour said. As if he could sense our annoyance, he quickly added: “I won’t tell anyone.”

Chapter 17: Swag

The Gi-Spot party was next week and I couldn't wait for Caden to fall in love with me, I mean, with my party planning prowess. I intercepted him (or pounced, as Sydney later described) at the coffee bar in the hopes of setting up a meeting with him to share Sydney's and my brilliant work in setting the party back on track.

"Just tell me that everything's perfect and I trust you," he smiled at me.

"It's all perfect," I responded, blushing and smiling shyly.

"Good, that's my girl," he winked.

"You're welcome," Sydney, who was standing beside me, added loudly.

"Sydney – wonderful that you can help out. We're in good hands with you. Listen ladies, I gotta dash. I have a meeting with Klaus. I'll put in a good word for you," Caden added with a wink.

I stood swooning in his beautiful aftermath while Sydney rolled her eyes. "Why does he wink so much? It's like he has a twitch."

"Oh come on, he's just being fun," I said, still gazing adoringly at the direction in which he left.

"If by fun you mean inappropriately flirtatious then yes, I would agree," Sydney said. "Snap out of it, girlfriend."

I laughed at her poor imitation of Stevie. "That was a horrible Stevie."

"I know," Sydney laughed. "I just can't do gay."

"I say we have an intervention. He hasn't RSVP'ed to the Gi-Spot party yet which is shocking. He better not even *think* of not coming."

"Stevie would never miss an opportunity to schmooze. All the Gisele Canada executives will be there. And the US GiGi executives too, so it's a good chance for you to get some face time if you want to go to New York."

In my quest to land Caden, I had almost forgotten about my initial goal to be transferred to New York. "How did you know that?" I asked, taken aback.

"I have my own Tracker. Mind of a steel trap." Sydney tapped her forehead. "I'm kidding. You used to talk about it. Don't you remember?"

"No," I said, frowning in slight bewilderment.

"Hey, don't let a man make you lose sight of your goals, much less a man you have no chance in hell with."

I grappled as to why I had forgotten about my New York objective. Was Caden distracting me from my ambitions or was I changing?

"I'm sorry, I couldn't help but overhear," the barista said, her face full of sheepish sympathy. "Caden hits on all the girls at the coffee bar, even me. It's kind of his thing. I'd be careful with him."

OMG, even the *barista* knows.

My heart plummeting down to the cute pair of heels I just bought, I changed the topic. "Have you seen Stevie lately? How is he doing?"

With the unsolicited blessings of my cube neighbour, Sydney and I recently ambushed Stevie in his office only to be shooed out by his Director who immediately followed us like a tracking device, a corporate version of the ol' ball and chain.

"I don't see him much anymore, only when I'm on the early shift. He runs in for a quick coffee-to-go. Poor guy."

"This is ridiculous, we need to disarm his Director and stage a stand-in at his office," I turned to Sydney.

"After the party," she said. "One thing at a time. You still need to take care of the swag bags."

"You're right. A party isn't a party without the swag," I replied with my newfound infinite wisdom of party planner extraordinaire.

If I couldn't resurrect Stevie's superstar reputation among his peers, perhaps I could resurrect my relationship with my girlfriends. Now that the Gi-spot party was under control, I could dedicate more time to making good for my bad behaviour. Also, enough time had gone by that I was no longer squeamish with embarrassment.

I called Calista, prepping myself to apologize profusely. Instead, she gave me a rather absurd and irrelevant lecture about a frog in boiling water.

"Am I the frog in this story?" I asked, unsure of whether I should be offended.

"Are you going to jump out or boil yourself alive?"

"This is very morbid," I commented. "But the Gi-Spot party is in a few days. I'd love for you to come."

There was a long silence on the line. "Hello?" I asked.

"Thanks, but I have no desire to go," Calista replied. "Good luck though."

"Are you mad at me?" I asked.

"I don't get it. Less than a year ago you wanted to save the world and now you're selling mascara that apparently gives people cancer."

"Well, that's not proven," I pointed out.

"Yeah, well, I hope it works out."

"OK, I'll call you after the party and let you know how it goes."

That was weird. I didn't know whether it was the PhD that had inspired Calista into talking in mysterious metaphors and bad omens but it was a little bit of a downer. It probably was best that she didn't come to the Gi-Spot party.

"We have a problem," I appeared frantically at Sydney's cube the day before the Gi-Spot party with a deja vu of my first Marketing Meeting we botched.

"Oh no. What else did Chloe eff up?" Sydney looked up calmly from her computer.

"It's not Chloe. Well, maybe just her bad luck charm. The products for the swag bag were supposed to arrive two days ago but they're held up at the border."

Sydney remained unfazed. "Believe it or not but this happens a lot because we're always so last minute. Try calling the customs office directly instead of going through FedEx."

After getting off the phone with the customs office and shamelessly promising the customs lady a shipment of our new Phat Lash mascara, I had to hand it to Sydney. She was really giving Stevie a run for his money. They were going to release the shipment first thing tomorrow morning.

To my relief, Stevie finally confirmed his attendance to the Gi-Spot party in person.

"Stevie, you've finally come out of hiding!" I exclaimed when he made a now rare personal appearance at my cube.

"Whatever are you whining about darling? Did you get my RSVP? I can't remember if I sent it."

"I didn't get it but I assumed you were coming because otherwise I would whip your ass." I pointed my finger at him in warning.

"Sounds like a good thing. Maybe I don't want to go anymore."

"Ew!" I laughed. Stevie's humour wasn't usually that crass. He sounded a bit like his horrible fiends Ruffian and Man Boobs.

"Put me out of my misery, what are you wearing to the party, my dear?"

"I think I'm going to wear that red DVF wrap dress I bought on our first shopping trip together. Remember, I wore it to the #1 Gisele party almost a year ago?"

Stevie looked horrified. "Wha – whaaaaat???" His voice rising to an alarming high pitch. "Are you sure you want to wear the same dress twice with the same audience?"

"No one remembers what I wore a year ago," I said. "And if they do, I'm worried." My response may have sounded confident but Stevie had planted the seed of panic in my heart.

"Well…at least it's very environmentally responsible of you," Stevie said, sounding unconvinced and mildly grossed out.

"Right. More like financially responsible. How are things?" I ventured to ask before he could convince me to invest in a new over-priced party dress.

"Swell, just super!" he responded gaily and with a *tah!* he was gone.

"He sounds fine," I said out loud to convince myself more so than my cube neighbour.

"When should I start freaking out?" I asked Sydney mid-afternoon when the products still hadn't arrived. The Gi-Spot party was set to start at 7 pm that evening.

"Why?" Sydney was leaving work early to get ready and arrive a couple of hours before the party started at Berkley Church to help set up.

"The products haven't arrived at the FedEx office yet."

"What?!" I hadn't seen Sydney this unsettled since I had mistakenly set up a makeup shrine in the wrong boardroom almost a year ago.

"How could you be so calm? You need to get on the phone with FedEx now!" Sydney's eyes were wide with panic. "Forget it, I'll do it." Sydney dumped her bag and pushed me out of the way to reach for my phone.

"Sydney, relax," I grabbed the phone from her. "I got it." Why was everyone losing it on me? First Stevie, then Calista, now Sydney. "Seriously, I got it."

She looked momentarily shocked at her uncharacteristic outburst and picked up her bag calmly. "Sorry, we put so much work into making this party happen, I just don't want to screw up now. Just bring the swag straight to the church and we'll pack the bags together. Here, take my car." She handed me her car keys. "I'll subway it."

My mouth dropped open in disbelief. "Your Mini? Seriously?"

Sydney nodded.

"Cool! I'm totally going to be like Charlize Theron in the *Italian Job*, racing through the streets in my Mini!"

"Well, not exactly during rush hour," Sydney pointed out. "The only thing that's going to be racing is your blood pressure."

"You're such a buzz kill," I pouted.

"Yeah, please don't speed in my car," Sydney advised me.

"You're really cool," I told her back as she left. It sounded sarcastic but I meant it. She turned her head and made a face.

Luckily, when I called FedEx, I spoke with a woman. All the easier to bribe her with makeup. The products were en route to arrive just before the FedEx office closed. I negotiated to keep the office open a half hour longer until 5:30 pm and raced over in Sydney's Mini. Well, more like raced out of the parking garage and then within seconds crawled at an agonizingly slow pace, caught in downtown rush hour traffic. I could have walked faster in my three inch heels and tight pencil skirt. I tried to squash visions from the Italian Job of the little Mini shooting down sidewalks and alleyways before they became a reality.

I grew fiercely jealous of pedestrians who seemed to be flying by on the sidewalks. I intensely hated all drivers around me for choosing to drive on this street at this time. I sent them evil wishes with my cut eye. Indeed, my blood pressure rose with my anger and frustration. I helplessly watched the clock climb closer to 5:30 pm.

After fifteen minutes of this unbearable non-activity, I realized with a panicked gasp that I would have to drive directly to Berkley

Church, leaving me no time to transform into a vixen. There was only one person who could rescue me from this dilemma. I called Stevie on his cell and work phones endlessly until he answered. Stevie, even whilst crashing and burning, could not resist a fashion emergency.

He finally picked up his work phone after my seventh attempt. "Darling, this better be an emergency."

"Worse, it's a *fashion* emergency!" The stress of sitting in traffic had amplified the urgency of my situation.

Stevie's gasp was a perfect match to my earlier gasp. He urged me to share my predicament. "I have the most fabu outfit in mind. Don't worry about the price – we'll leave the tags on and you can return it later if you don't love it. But trust me honey, you're gonna love it. What size are you again?"

"I'm a 2!" I exclaimed in excitement.

There was a pregnant pause on the other line. "I'm a 6," I corrected, my excitement deflating momentarily.

"OK, meet you at the church at 6:00 pm."

"Thanks Stevie. You're the best." I breathed a deep sigh of relief and inhaled a lungful of traffic smog and congestion. A taxi driver cut me off, as suddenly as one can when traveling at five miles an hour. "Watch it, asshole!" I yelled, my blood boiling. Luckily, all the windows were up to protect me from detection and retaliation.

"Where are you?" Stevie's tone reflected his gentlemanly distaste of my unnecessarily loud profanity.

"Oh, I'm just sitting in traffic. It's horrible. Can you stay on the phone and keep me company?"

"No."

I arrived at the FedEx office an excruciating two minutes before it closed, parked illegally and dashed as quickly as I could in my three inch heels into the building. The FedEx lady I had bribed with makeup helped me load the seven heavy boxes into my car. I ripped open a box and offered her a few handfuls of makeup, which she accepted, acting surprised, as if she had pulled a favour solely out of the goodness of her heart. She described the shortest route to Berkley Church and I attempted to race off only to be halted to a dead stop, once again by traffic. I banged my head against the steering wheel.

When I finally arrived at Berkley Church, it was quarter past six which gave us only forty-five minutes to pack two hundred swag bags and make me gorgeous, the latter likely taking longer given my frenzied state. Sydney and Stevie greeted me outside and helped me haul the boxes of swag to the basement. They had devised a packing strategy and had accordingly set up the swag bags into rows. We sorted the products into separate boxes and formed an efficient assembly line, packing the swag bags in record time. Ecstatic with our mad swag-bag packing skills, we high-fived each other and ran the swag bags triumphantly up to the event planners who joined our cheering. We collectively celebrated as if we had just found out that all the swag was actually for us.

We got shushed by a senior manager from the event planning company. While we were slaving away in the church basement, Caden was being interviewed by MTV. He was strategically standing in front of the Gi-Spot branded makeup stations. A gaggle of female bartenders and servers posed behind him, bound in intimidating dominatrix gear. He was confident and completely at ease in front of the bright lights and cameras. I stared at him as he charmed the crew as effortlessly as he had allured me. Even at a distance I was captivated by his gorgeous manliness.

"It's beautiful, isn't it?" One of the event planners asked.

I snapped out of my reverie, embarrassed to have been caught openly lusting over my boss, but then realized that she was talking about the venue. I looked beyond Caden and realized that the event planners had done a phenomenal job at transforming Berkley Church into their vision of the Seven Deadly Sins. It was stunning – dark, twisted and edgy.

"It's amazing," I agreed, nodding in admiration. My praise was cut short when Stevie and Sydney grabbed me and pulled me into a bathroom to get ready.

The party dress that Stevie had purchased for me was breathtaking and fit me perfectly.

"Stevie!" I gushed, admiring the dress in the mirror. "It's so hot!"

"You're hot! Just don't look at the price tag," he winced. Sydney had heated up a curling iron while I was changing and Stevie demonstrated his unexpected hair styling prowess, as he expertly curled my hair into soft waves. "Frederico is going to do your makeup."

"Who's Frederico?" I asked.

"You don't know who Frederico is?" Stevie asked, shocked. I looked at Sydney's reflection in the mirror to confirm whether I was living under a rock and she shook her head and shrugged. "Frederico is pure genius. He's the Makeup Director of GiGi Cosmetics. It's an honour that he can perform at this event for us."

"Oh, well…wow, thanks. How did you manage to get him to do my makeup?"

He smiled and winked at me.

"Oh my gosh, Stevie, what did you do?" I asked, looking at Sydney with concern.

"Don't worry, I didn't sleep with him," he rolled his eyes and then giggled. "Not that I don't want to."

"Shame on you for having such sinful thoughts in a church," Sydney teased.

"What about Jamie?" I asked, practically outraged.

Stevie shrugged.

"What does that mean?" My outrage growing.

"Enough about me," Stevie set down the curling iron and fluffed my hair. "Gorgeous girl." Stevie, hands on hip and head cocked, admired his work like a proud prom parent.

"Way to change the topic," I assented.

"We gotta go. You clean up good, kid. Just one last thing," Sydney spritzed a recognizable fragrance in the air and made me walk through it. It was my favourite smell – bull shit.

"Vanity's *stressful!*" I proclaimed as we exited the bathroom and linked arms to join the party.

Chapter 18: Party

WHILE IT WAS CERTAINLY NOT enough to turn me on, Stevie was right that Frederico was pure makeup genius. Frederico was fun and wild, in an overtly gay Latino way. And with a name like Frederico, you'd better be fun and wild. Despite his Latino flavour, I was surprised that Stevie was so enamoured by him. He did not seem to be Stevie's type, and makeup genius aside, he was no match for Jamie. I did not approve.

As my face progressed into a level of vixen I could only dream of, so did the level of Stevie and Frederico's shameless flirting, to the point where I felt uncomfortable to be seated in between them.

"OK, guys, you need to get a room," I finally said, squirming in my seat.

Stevie responded with a raucously loud and fake laugh as he pounded me on the shoulder. "Oh, Veronica, Frederico is in a long-term and loving relationship with Hunter, the Makeup Director for Gisele. I swear, could you dream of a more wonderful couple?"

Frederico raised a sculpted eyebrow.

"Just like you're in a loving relationship with Jamie," I replied. I turned to Frederico to reinforce the statement. "He's in a loving relationship with Jamie."

"Keep still, keep still, darling, and go like this with your lips," he smacked his lips together in an over-exaggerated fashion and what I hoped to be extremely unattractive to Stevie. "Hunter and I are no longer together. It is tragic but I hope to never see him again. It would not be pretty." His eyes darkened. Next stop: check tonight's roster of makeup artists to ensure Hunter is not on the list.

"Oh no!" Stevie gasped, hand to his heart.

"There, you are done and you are gorgeous, my love," Frederico spun me around so that I could admire his work in the mirror. Now both Stevie and I had our hands to our hearts. I noticed the word *Vanity* above his makeup station spelled out in an embellished handwriting script in tiny Swarovski crystals.

"Stevie was right, you are a makeup god."

Stevie and Frederico beamed at one another. "Hey, eyes on the prize," I snapped at Stevie. Now I knew what it felt like for Stevie and Sydney to distract me from Caden.

"Oh, Veronica, you're so needy," Stevie joked at my expense. "You're gorgeous, you're gorgeous. How many times must you hear it to believe it?" He held up his hands in exasperation and looked at Frederico like a puppy dog desperate for his master's attention.

"How about you tell me some more as we have a drink at the bar?" I asked.

"Beauty comes from the inside and radiates out," Frederico said. Indeed, ironic words from a makeup artist. "There is nothing more beautiful than a confident woman when she smiles."

"Right, tell that to my boss," I laughed. Frederico pointed to my smile in approval.

"Ronnie, you go ahead without me, I'm going to try and soak in more of Frederico's genius. Teach me!" Stevie made bowing worshipping gestures in the direction of Frederico.

This was certainly worrisome. There were very few things that Stevie favoured to free alcohol.

I joined Heidi and her entourage, Chloe and Jasmine Tit, already paying respects to *Gluttony*, affixed above the bar in a rope of black velvet.

As soon as Chloe saw me, her frown deepened. "Ugh, it's so hot in here, I'm sweating like a whore in church!"

"You said it, not me," I replied. I thought I saw Heidi stifle a laugh.

"Congratulations, it looks great," Heidi offered me an uncharacteristic compliment in front of her entourage. Her makeup was so natural that I wondered whether she forgot to apply it.

"Oh please, do you think Veronica has anything to do with this?" Chloe practically snarled. The drink in her hand sloshed over the side of the glass and Heidi had to swerve out of the way to avoid getting splashed. "The event planners did everything."

"Chloe, did you remember to take your medication today?" Sydney appeared beside me. "Seriously, I have something that can take the edge off."

"My boyfriend says that painkillers are the most addictive drug," Jasmine piped up. We all stopped and looked at Jasmine Tit with confusion.

"Really? Is that what your boyfriend says?" Chloe exploded. "I'm so sick of hearing what your stupid boyfriend thinks! What do *you* think? Do you even have an opinion or a mind of your own? If I wanted to know what your boyfriend thinks, I'd ask him. But I don't. You know why? Because I don't give a shit what he thinks!"

The world was suspended for a moment as we all looked at Jasmine Tit with wide eyes and bated breath for her response. Jasmine Tit inhaled deeply and stood a little taller. "Well, I just thought it was a nice way of saying that you have a serious problem with painkillers."

Our mouths all dropped open simultaneously.

"They make you such a bitch," Jasmine Tit added, as if what she said previously didn't make enough of an impact. I noted the gaping absence of '*my boyfriend thinks*' at the beginning of the sentence.

"This is *awesome*," Sydney said under her breath.

"It explains a lot," I agreed, also under my breath, and then added loudly: "We're going to go. This is probably, you know, a private conversation."

Sydney looked at me, disappointed, rooted to the spot.

"We need to attend to an emergency," I motioned to Sydney. She followed me grudgingly, and I filled her in on the Frederico-Hunter situation.

"Beware the wrath of a gay makeup artist scorned," she agreed.

"Speaking of gay scorn, could you check on Stevie? I'm worried that he's going to do something stupid with Frederico."

"Stevie's a big boy, he can take care of himself," Sydney dismissed my concern. "Besides, Frederico's a professional. He needs to work this event."

"I don't know…"

I flagged an event planner, easily identifiable sporting a headset and clip board, and asked her whether Hunter was scheduled to work the event. Unfortunately he was, but fortunately he was running late. I instructed that Hunter be escorted directly to the makeup table the furthest away from Frederico. The event planner nodded and scurried away as if high profile gay makeup artist breakups were a normal occurrence in her line of work.

"I hope we can keep them apart the whole time," I asked Sydney, growing uneasy about the potentially disastrous encounter.

"I got it," Sydney assured me and left me on her quest to fend off the Frederico-Hunter showdown.

I stood off to the side for a moment to enjoy the fruits of my labour. The church had already filled up with the city's most beautiful and well-dressed young socialites. Despite the abundance of beautiful people all around, I noticed that a few men were checking me out. Wow, Frederico really was a magician. I smiled confidently and played flirtatiously with my hair. My inner beauty must really be radiating out. It wasn't often that I was the object of men's admiration so I might as well enjoy it. I realized in my confident woman glory that quite a few men were now unabashedly staring at me. Hmmm…this was a little too unusual. I looked down. Was my dress see-through? Was a boob hanging out?

I turned around and realized that I was standing in front of a massive screen that was playing the GiGi soft porn TV ad. It seemed that I was blocking it and in fact men were staring at me, but in the hopes that I would get the hell out of the way. I gingerly stepped out of the way, appropriately humbled. I was standing uncomfortably off to the side when Sydney came to fetch me for the fashion show which was already set to begin. Wow, time flies when you're humiliated.

Sydney and I headed upstairs to get a good position in front of the runway. The word Envy was emblazoned above the runway in bright lights. I spotted Caden, surrounded by an unlovely display of women who were smothering him with their fake boobs, desperate flirtation and mindless giggles. It was so obvious, they practically had dollar signs in their eyes. Somehow, he did not seem to mind. I reserved a spot for Sydney and me at the end of the runway as she grabbed drinks for us at the upstairs bar.

"I hope they fixed the runway," Sydney told me, handing me a martini glass. "During the dress rehearsal the models were slipping everywhere."

My eyes widened as the lights dimmed to complete darkness. Oh God, another potential disaster – model down. Someone screamed as an immature joke. There was spotty laughter throughout the room. Rock music suddenly blasted and spotlights simultaneously hit the runway, flooding it with white hot light. One spotlight was quite unstrategically directed right into the eyeline of the models. They strutted, blinded, down the runway, happily unaware of how close they were coming to walking off the end of it. I prayed every time a model came alarmingly close to the edge that she stop. Many of them tested my faith by stopping within inches of the end of the runway. I was poised to catch their frail little bodies if they careened over the edge.

Not only were the blinded models freaking me out, but sure to Sydney's warning, the models were slipping in their slick-soled stiletto heels. Some shoes were too big and their little toothpick legs were wobbling as they fought to keep their shoes on. I hoped I was the only one that noticed these glitches because I was painfully aware of it. Sydney and I gasped and grabbed each other's hands as one model, outfitted in a gorgeous evening dress, turned to walk off the runway stage left and took a headfirst plunge backstage. All we saw was crinoline and heels in the air. I looked furtively around to see if anyone else noticed.

I heard glass breaking and winced, praying there was no blood. Happily, someone had broken their martini glass all over the eye-level runway. I immediately had visions of models stomping on the broken glass and shards flying into the faces of eager onlookers, I shoved all the beautiful people out of my way, admittedly unnecessarily roughly, to find an event planner. I flagged down the same event planner that helped ward off the clash of the scorned gay ex-lovers. As calmly as if I had told her there was the threat of a gay ex-lover apocalyptic showdown, she radioed back stage to tell the models to avoid the broken glass and then radioed security to push the people away from that section of the runway.

If only I could radio in to the higher powers that be to clean up all my life's screw-ups and regrets. Veronica to Lord Almighty. Messy break-up last night. Please erase inappropriate comments about lovemaking skills from ex-boyfriend's memory. Veronica out. "Where can I get one of those?" I pointed to her headset.

She laughed. "Thanks, good catch with the broken glass."

"I don't know how you do this and maintain a healthy blood pressure." I yelled back.

"I love every minute of it," she gushed. "It's like an adrenaline rush!"

I was envious that at such a young age she had landed a job that she was truly passionate about. I wish I could say the same of my job. My job was a means to an end and the only thing I was passionate about, I realized, was the end.

I scanned the room for Caden. If I couldn't enjoy the party, at least I could enjoy Caden enjoying the party. And there he was – enjoying the women enjoying him at the party. Protected by the darkness, I stared at him talking intimately with a woman who seemed to be a doppelgänger of his last girlfriend. I made a face. It seemed Caden had a type and it was Gross Barbie Doll.

"You have a hot boss," the event planner had noticed my not-so inconspicuous staring.

Jolted out of my shameless love trance, I tore my eyes away from Caden and the Gross Barbie Doll. "Yeah," I replied as nonchalantly as I could.

"Two words for you: Don't date him girl dot com."

I blinked. "Those are like, five words."

"No, it's a web site. Dontdatehimgirl.com. Check it out. He's on it – there's twenty pages from like, seven ex-girlfriends dedicated to him."

I swallowed. "Well, you can't believe everything you read, especially from pissed off ex-girlfriends."

She shrugged. "Read it. Judge for yourself."

When the show was over I bolted over to Caden to convince him that there were more attractive women in the world than Gross Barbie Dolls.

He was still talking to the ex-girlfriend doppelgänger so I felt it was appropriate to rudely interrupt.

"Caden, how are you enjoying the party? Hi, I'm Veronica. I work for Caden," I introduced myself to the Gross Barbie Doll.

"Hi, I'm Britney," she shook my hand limply and I almost shuddered. There are few things more disturbing than a lifeless hand shake.

"Oh…"

"No, this is a different Britney," Caden interjected smoothly, accurately reading my confused expression.

I couldn't help myself from making a face. "Seriously?" So if I wanted to date Caden, I would have to get a disproportionately large boob job, dye my hair blonde, lose several million brain cells *and* change my name to Britney?

"Veronica, you look absolutely beautiful tonight," Caden smiled. "And you have completely outdone yourself with this party. It's tremendous and I'm so proud of you."

My grimace soon melted into a loving gaze. "Thank you," I gushed.

"You know you're my favourite, right?" he continued. I smiled shyly. "So, I hope it's OK if I ask you a huge favour."

"Anything!"

"It's Chloe," he responded and my smile vanished. "She drank too much and I think she's sick in the bathroom. I don't want her to embarrass herself so can you escort her out and make sure no one sees her in this state?"

"Uh…" I racked my brain for an excuse. "What about her friends? I'm not sure she would listen to me."

"No," he frowned. "She seems to have gotten into a fight with her girlfriends and they don't want to talk to her right now."

"Nice friends," I said.

"Please, I don't want her to make a scene and ruin all the hard work you've done."

"OK," I assented. I would rather break up a Frederico – Hunter showdown than drag a puking Chloe out of a church. Sure enough, I found Chloe locked in a bathroom stall. Surprisingly, I heard sobbing instead of the sound of wretched puking. I didn't know what was worse – a puking Chloe or a rabid bi-polar Chloe.

I hesitated and grimaced before I called out her name. "Chloe?" Chloe stopped sobbing but did not answer.

"Chloe, I know you're in there," I called out again. She didn't respond. I hoped desperately that she hadn't choked on her puke or other such things that pill-popping drunkards are apt do.

"Chloe? Are you OK?"

"Go away," she finally said and started sobbing again. I rolled my eyes.

"I know, this totally sucks for me too, trust me, but I'm trying to help you get home. Do you want to go home or do you want to sleep in the bathroom stall?" I felt like I was cajoling a child. This better get me higher on The Tracker.

"It's bad for your skin," I added after another long silence. "You'll probably break out the next day."

Chloe clumsily unlocked the door. She was seated on the closed-lid toilet and slumped against the wall of the bathroom stall. Her makeup was completely ruined, black streaks of mascara running down her face, forming little black rivers cutting through the many layers of foundation, blush and powder.

"Uh…are you OK?" This was worse than I thought. I didn't know how to handle a alcohol/drug-induced meltdown.

"I'm stupid," she mumbled incoherently. "Stupid."

"We've all drunk too much and gotten our friends mad at us. Trust me. It just happened to me," I said, handing her some tissues to wipe her face. Her eyes were barely open. After shaking the tissues in front of her face uselessly, I placed them in her lap. "Come on, there are cabs waiting outside." I clapped, as if she were a dog I was trying to potty train.

"No, I don't want to…see me…this," she hiccuped through her sobs. "Stupid…hate me."

"It's OK, I won't let anyone see you," I lied. "Do you need help getting up?"

She remained slumped on the toilet.

"What in the world?" It was the serendipitously-appearing event planner. I swear, they hired her just to follow me around in anticipation that disaster would do the same.

"Oh, thank God. You're my new best friend. Do you think she's all right?"

The event planner surveyed her for a moment. "Yeah," she finally said in a nonchalant manner that, had I cared, would not have instilled much confidence in me.

"Good, can you help me put her in a cab? "

"I'll call security."

"Um, can you be discreet about it? She works for Gisele and it might be career limiting if someone sees her like this."

"No, problem, we'll take her down the back staircase," she responded as breezily as if I told her there was broken glass on the eye-level runway at risk of being kicked into someone's eyes.

If someone had told me a week ago that I would be covering Chloe's ass, I would have told them they were a rabid, pill-popping drunkard.

Chapter 19: Thank You

With Chloe dutifully sent home in a cab, and hopefully lucid enough to remember her address, I re-entered the party and was greeted by a topless and very buff male model carrying a tray of sushi. With a nod to the dominatrix-outfitted waitresses, he sported a studded collar. He had the handwritten word *Lust* inscribed across his overly oiled chest in what I hoped was a fake tattoo. He looked like he was cast from the last Gay Pride Parade. I did not find nudity and raw fish to be a particularly savoury combination but stuffed my face with sushi nonetheless.

And with sushi practically busting out of my mouth, I saw Caden looking at me for acknowledgement that I had completed my unpleasant assignment. I covered my mouth and gave him a thumbs up. He seemed to sigh in relief and put his hands together in a prayer position, bowing his head to me and mouthing the words *thank you*. I smiled as much as my sushi-packed mouth would allow and was relieved to observe that he had moved on from wooing his Gross Barbie Doll companion to networking with the Gisele suits.

I passed by the *Vanity* makeup stations and was dismayed to see Stevie still clinging to Frederico like Jasmine Tit to her boyfriend's every word. Stevie was watching Frederico, enraptured, explain his art as he transformed his latest subject to a thing of beauty.

"Hey Stevie, how are you enjoying the party?" I joined the threesome at the makeup station.

"Tremendously. Almost as much I'm enjoying Frederico's talents," Stevie cooed.

"Wow, it's so hot in here...it must really be irritating your rash..." I yelled loudly.

Stevie shot me a panicked look. "What rash? Where?"

"Oh! Sorry, I didn't mean to say anything in front of...Don't worry, it's not contagious," I told Frederico. "It looks like...*wow*, but it just flares up when, um... he's hot." I motioned all over my torso with my hands. "All over."

"Ronnie! What in God's name are you talking about?" Stevie was rightfully outraged.

"Funny story," I laughed to Frederico, keeping my voice at an unnecessarily high volume. "He can't treat it with medication because it interferes with all the other prescription drugs he's on. You know, for all his other crazy ailments."

Frederico laughed, brushing off my attempts to undermine Stevie's appeal. Judging by her alarmed eyes, it managed to disgust the person currently getting her makeup done by Frederico.

"What the hell, Ronnie?" Stevie was livid. "You can go now. Thanks."

I slunk away defeated, my good intentions surely paving my path closer to hell. I saw Oompa Loompa gesturing emphatically to me to join him and Savannah by the bar. Oompa Loompa looked like he was in a very celebratory spirit. Even in the dim lighting, I could tell that his face was bright red and perspiring. Savannah looked severely bored.

"Congratulations, Veronica, this is a tour de force," Oompa Loompa engulfed me with praise.

Savannah nodded hesitatingly in agreement.

"Don't look so stressed! This is a party!" Oompa Loompa motioned to the scary looking S&M bartender for another drink. "And it is quite the party. Very impressive. I doubt the parties are this good in *New York*." He winked at me, contorting his face to squish his left eye closed.

"Oh…it was nothing," I shrugged and shook my head, overcome with modesty, an unfortunate female tendency at this moment. "It was mostly the event planners. I can't take the credit."

"Nonsense!" Oompa Loompa boomed.

Savannah's eyes narrowed as she surveyed my reaction, making me uneasy.

Oompa Loompa motioned Klaus over with the exaggerated motions of one who has consumed too much alcohol. I felt myself grow nervous enough to suddenly crave a Jägerbomb. I had wrestled over my worthiness, intelligence and competence for weeks after my last interaction with Klaus.

"Fantastic party," Klaus approached. He smiled and nodded approvingly at a bare-chested and Lust-tattooed waiter carrying a tray of martinis. The waiter's steroid-induced muscles were so lubed up, I hoped the tray wouldn't slip from his greasy hands. Klaus's gaze remained on the waiter for awhile as we stood awkwardly waiting.

Once Klaus lost sight of the lubricated waiter, he turned and greeted us gregariously. He grabbed my hand and shook it emphatically. "Congratulations, Veronica."

My expression frozen in surprise like that of the over-Botoxed Celeste, I was speechless. I didn't know that Klaus remembered my existence, much less knew my name.

"*Fliegender Hirsch*!" Klaus yelled to the bartendress and motioned to all of us by spinning a pointed index finger towards the heavens. She shook her head, confused. "*Fliegender Hirsch*!" he kept repeating, exasperated, wringing his hands in the air.

"It means Jägerbomb," Savannah, apparently fluent in German frat party drinks, leaned in discreetly towards me. "Pretend you don't know."

"Really?" I asked, excited. Maybe Klaus and I would get along after all. "I mean, that's disgusting."

"It's vile," she shuddered. "What kind of sadist would think of mixing the two most disgusting liquids on earth?" I could think of a few more disgusting liquids I would rather not drink, such as urine and phlegm for example, but decided it wise not to share.

"I guess good marketing could sell anything," I said.

"We're fools," she responded.

A dramatist, Klaus decided on flaming Sambuca, a pale comparison to the Jägerbomb, but decidedly easier to stomach than urine and phlegm. He offered a toast to the success of Gi-Spot.

"I hope our Gi-Spot is as successful as your party," he declared with a poorly chosen adjective and uncharacteristic praise, brought on perhaps by the Sambuca.

"I'm glad you're enjoying it." I responded, again made shy with modesty. In any case, I suspected that he enjoyed most parties, as long as they had a well-stocked bar and partially nude men. "A party is only as good as the people who attend."

"Yes, this is a very beautiful, sexy party," he approved. "The foundation of the essence of Gisele."

I nodded, not sure of how to respond to his proclamation.

"I would like to introduce you to my friends from New York. Please excuse me for a moment." Klaus left, leaving me alone with Savannah. Oompa Loompa had moved on to befriend the next group of innocent bystanders.

"You talk too much," she said after a moment of self conscious silence.

I said nothing as I felt it was the most appropriate response to her comment.

"Just say thank you," she continued.

"Thank you?" I questioned obediently.

"When someone pays you a compliment, just shut up and say thank you. Don't start talking – you're a train wreck."

"Oh…I guess I'm too modest."

"Modesty doesn't become your career," she replied, her face showing her disgust. "It's infuriating. When someone gives you credit for something, take it, damn it! Don't start giving them crap like the people make the party. Please!"

Klaus approached us with two suits in tow. They were surprisingly young, no doubt from their loyalty to Gisele's anti-aging elixirs.

"That's the VP of GiGi North America and the Director of Gisele North America. Remember, two words: thank you. Don't say anything else."

"OK," I nodded, humbled by her severe advice.

"Veronica, please meet Monsieur Williams and Monsieur Davis." I supposed the higher in stature you were at Gisele, the more appropriate the use of French for your title, regardless of whether or not you spoke a word of French. I shook their hands, endeavouring to appear esteemed to be in their presence.

"Wonderful party," one suit said.

"Great job," the other suit added.

"Thank you," I said, grateful to have been fed a simple script by Savannah.

"This is every bit the same quality as the GiGi launch party in New York," one suit admitted, almost grudgingly. "I didn't know there were so many beautiful people in Toronto."

"Thank you," I replied, albeit probably not the most suitable response, from their suddenly furrowed brows.

"Have you met your US counterparts? You should exchange learnings with them."

"Thank you," I replied robotically, fearing that they would soon find me incredibly boring.

"Have you met your US counterparts?" he repeated.

I contemplated a sensible response for a moment but then stuck stubbornly to Savannah's advice: "Thank you."

I saw Savannah sigh and shake her head, irritated.

"Apologies Monsieur, it's loud in here," she jumped in. "Veronica hasn't had a chance yet to meet her US colleagues, she's been busy working hard on the Gi-Spot launch party and the Phat Lash launch."

"Well, get her down there. We'd love to have her."

I smiled, amazed at my good fortune. "Thank you." And I must say, that was the perfect response to the perfect question.

Apocalyptic disasters averted, Gisele suits duly impressed (with the party, not my conversational abilities) and with full trust in the divine powers behind the event planners' headsets, I set out to enjoy my party.

Not surprisingly, Mateo had practiced enough gluttonous alcohol consumption to deem it suitable to heat up the dance floor. I eagerly scanned the surrounding area for Heidi's reaction. She was still with him so no doubt she had not yet witnessed his testosterone-stripping habit. It was admittedly evil of me to eagerly anticipate Heidi's distress at discovering a potentially catastrophic flaw in her romantic partner, but I did not want to miss it.

Heidi was standing at the edge of the dance floor with Jasmine Tit, perhaps sharing her autonomously-derived thoughts on the party. I joined them as Mateo was warming up with The Robot.

"Hi!" I greeted them. "No worries, Chloe's OK."

They looked back blankly at me.

"She was sick in the bathroom," I explained.

"Chloe was sick?" Heidi looked surprised. "When she drinks too much, she always takes off without saying goodbye so we figured she just left."

"I hope she got home OK," Jasmine Tit said. "I usually get my boyfriend to drive her home." They appeared to be genuinely concerned but I found it odd that they had refused Caden's request to help Chloe and now made no mention of it.

"Does she cry when she…uh…drinks too much?" I asked.

"Cry?" There was a flicker of guilt across Jasmine Tit's otherwise stony expression.

"What the hell?!" Heidi exclaimed in outrage. I gleefully looked towards the dance floor. Mateo had added an unfortunate dance move to his repertoire. It was a frenetic grind/hip thrust performed off beat to the music. The unlucky recipients of his hips' aggressive conquest was a group of good-looking girls carefully attired in this season's most coveted fashion mandatories. They scattered like models away from a dessert platter.

"What the *hell* is Matthew doing?" Heidi exclaimed again.

"I don't know, it looks like he's having some sort of an epileptic attack," Jasmine Tit said. I couldn't tell from her steely expression whether she was being sarcastic. "Should we call for help?"

"That's just the way he dances," I replied. "The only help he needs is a dance coach."

"Oh, he should worry all right," Heidi warned and stormed the dance floor, pushing the recent recipients of Mateo's hip pumps out of her way. I hadn't anticipated that Mateo's inferior dance moves would inspire such wrath from Heidi and was now not so sure I would enjoy the confrontation.

"Heidi used to take ballet," Jasmine Tit explained to me, incorrectly assessing Heidi's reaction.

Heidi grabbed Mateo's arm to spin him around and furiously devoured his face in an aggressively ugly kiss. They made out violently to the distaste of those on the dance floor who backed away for fear of injury from the brute force of their embrace.

Jasmine Tit was consumed in shock, her usually pursed lips gaping open in horror.

"Well! I did *not* expect that," I said by way of breaking the uncomfortable silence as we stared at the unapologetic display. "Who knew that bad dancing was such a turn on?" The predatory nature of their smooching was rather disturbing.

"Ew," Jasmine Tit closed her eyes in disgust and turned her face away from the unsettling sight.

The couple stopped to breathe and ensure no oral injuries. Mateo pumped his fist in the air and hollered to all around, "My girlfriend's hot!" He lifted her up and spun her around. "She's my girlfriend!"

"Girlfriend?" Jasmine Tit cried out in dismay, her face crumpling into a horrified grimace.

"Look how cute they are now," I said. He was twirling Heidi around innocently, if not ungracefully, around the dance floor.

"But…but he's so…" And unable to find the appropriate description without the help of her boyfriend, she shook her head in denial. "*Ew*!"

Not to be upstaged, Oompa Loompa entered the dance floor to show everyone how Oompa Loompas dance. Apparently they dance to the tune of Ukraine folk dancing. To the unexpected delight of the crowd, who promptly parted like the Red Sea, Oompa Loompa demonstrated his unlikely athletic abilities as he crouched low to the ground and kicked his legs out repeatedly. A lively crowd quickly formed to cheer on Oompa Loompa's impressive talents. Mateo clumsily attempted to join Oompa Loompa only to be met with boos within moments of displaying his curious lack of rhythm or sense of natural movement. He quickly retreated to allow Oompa Loompa the deserved glory of the dance floor.

Before Jasmine Tit could say "*Ew!*", Oompa Loompa was lifted on to the shoulders of men who bounced him around appreciatively. The party carried on in such a manner for the next couple of hours until the bar closed. Sydney had discovered the massage therapy stations early on in the evening and had disappeared from the festivities as she alternated treatments between massage therapists. She left the party early, induced into a comatose state from hours of indulgent back massages. The last of the swag had long ago been greedily depleted. I retreated to the basement to check if we had had the foresight to save any extra swag.

There were only left over cardboard boxes used to transport the swag. After months of intense labour, a few cardboard boxes were all that remained of the party, like a poor man's glass slipper. I felt strangely sad that the party was over and wondered whether the Phat Lash launch would be as harrowing an assignment.

"There you are." I heard a voice behind me and my heart fluttered as I recognized Caden's voice. I turned as he approached me. "I didn't get a chance to congratulate you for a fantastic job. I couldn't have done it better myself."

"Thank you," I said, my pulse quickening as he stopped a little too close in front of me.

"Thank *you*," he repeated, smiling. I looked up at him, feeling vulnerable by his unusual proximity to me.

"We work well together," he said. "We have great chemistry."

I blinked, surprised but delighted at his bold statement. "Oh… uh…"

"Don't you think?" he asked.

I nodded. He leaned in and stopped, his lips barely grazing mine.

"Veronica," I heard the chilling voice of Savannah. Caden sprang back. I quickly picked up the cardboard boxes, a weak cover-up for the obvious interaction that had preceded. "I've been looking for you." She stood with an icy expression, at the door. Her head of snakes had returned, snarling.

I stood speechless, heart pounding and blushing furiously.

"We're just finishing up down here," Caden recovered smoothly from Savannah's regrettably timed interruption. "Cleaning up." He nodded towards me, as I stood holding the cardboard boxes, covering my body as if ashamed. I nodded weakly.

"Interesting. I didn't know you were that hands-on, Caden," Savannah remarked in a cold voice. She remained motionless in the doorway observing us as a snake lunged from her head. The other snakes were coiling ominously about her head as they flickered their tongues at us.

"I am," he smiled good-naturedly. They looked at each other for a few moments. The snakes settled down but continued to glower at us menacingly.

"Well, Veronica, it's time to go," she said, still looking at Caden. "Great job and thank you for hard work."

"Am I fired?" I asked, humiliated.

"Fired? Don't be ridiculous. Now go home and get some rest. See you at work tomorrow morning."

Chapter 20: Rumours

After a listless night of sleep, I arrived at work the next morning, makeup missing and hair undone. With guilt and dread weighing on my chest, I knocked on Savannah's office door. The snakes were present but calm. She nodded for me to enter.

I sat down, bereft of speech from embarrassment. I looked down at my fingers fidgeting in my lap.

"I saw the whole thing," she spoke before I could start apologizing profusely. "I had my eye on him all evening and when I saw him follow you to the basement, I followed him."

"I'm sorry," I said, my face wrought with guilt. "Nothing…happened."

"Caden has a bit of a reputation and you are…" Savannah searched for the most fitting word, "…a very impressionable young lady. You're stupid but not to blame."

"Am I in trouble?" I asked after an agonizing silence.

"I trust that this won't happen again?" she asked.

"No, no," I promised her vehemently. "Is Caden in trouble?"

"You shouldn't worry about anyone but yourself. Do you understand how close you came to negating all your hard work? We're done here."

I nodded and got up to leave.

"One more thing, Veronica."

"Yes?" I winced and turned to face her.

"You are no longer on the Gi-Spot assignment, of course."

I nodded again as if it pained me.

Despite Savannah's warnings, I wanted desperately to talk about what happened in the basement with Caden. Despite my embarrassment, I was agonizing over Caden's consistently bad reputation and my feelings for him.

Stevie was waiting for me at my cube. And if I wasn't already feeling sufficiently mortified, I remembered my unchivalrous behaviour to keep Stevie away from Frederico last night.

"Stevie," I said. "I'm so sorry about the rash thing. I don't know what got into me. It wasn't my place."

"You were right," he said.

"Oh no," I said.

"Not about the rash but about Frederico," he quickly clarified. "Sydney asked me to keep Frederico away from Hunter."

"I see. Well, that lacked a bit of foresight," I replied. "It was brilliantly stupid."

"I'm brilliantly stupid. I was so afraid of screwing up with Jamie so I went ahead and did it anyway."

"Are you going to tell him?" I asked.

"I have to 'fess up," he said miserably. "The guilt would kill me. I'm doomed."

"I didn't know you were Catholic," came my feeble attempt at a joke.

"Catholic Poster Boy," he laughed meekly. "Listen," he lowered his voice. "I need to tell you something. I…uh…you know I don't like Caden, but I'm just telling you this because I care and I'm worried."

"Stevie," I sighed. "I know."

He looked surprised. "You know about Caden and Chloe?"

"What?"

"Oh…I guess not…" he realized. "I'm sorry to tell you this but he's such bad news…you need to stay away from him."

I gulped for air, my breathing laboured. "Caden and *Chloe*? How do you know this?"

"Last night, I went down to the basement to set up for the swag bags and they were down there. I heard voices so I stopped to listen outside. I shouldn't have." He shook his head and my stomach turned. "He was ending things with her. She was crying and begging and telling him she loved him. He threatened to go to HR and have her fired if she told anyone. It was awful."

I was disgusted by the thought of Caden and Chloe.

"Veronica, that could have been you."

"Did he catch you listening in?" I asked.

"I don't know. I only had time to run up the stairs and pretend I was just coming down. I played dumb." He smiled sheepishly. "Easy for me to do."

My phone rang. The call display showed that it was Caden. I mouthed *"It's him"* to Stevie who shook his head. "Don't answer it," he told me.

I gingerly picked up the phone. "Hello?"

"Veronica, I feel awful about last night," Caden said. "Please know that I would never do anything to make you feel uncomfortable."

"Don't worry about it," I said in a low voice while looking at Stevie who was intently studying my reactions.

"Do you have a minute right now? Let's talk."

"I'll be right over." I hung up the phone and despite the pleas of Stevie, I immediately headed to his office, wishing that I had taken the time to put on some makeup.

I knocked on his door hesitantly. "Hi," I said, standing uncomfortably in the door way.

"Hi," he smiled at me and leaned back in his chair, still undeniably gorgeous. "Come in. Close the door."

I closed the door and entered carefully.

"Veronica," he laughed. "Please don't look so nervous. It's me."

"I'm sorry, it's just awkward," I said, sitting down. I stared sadly at his face. I wished that I could stop loving the way he looked.

"It's exactly like that. Veronica, you're attractive but I'm your VP and it would be inappropriate."

"Yeah, you're right," I agreed. "Nothing happened, so it's no big deal. That's what I told Savannah."

"Good."

I was dismayed by the relief in his voice. How could I have missed what was so obvious to everyone else? Regardless of what I now knew, he still looked like a perfectly charming gentleman to me.

"I mean it's good that this won't get in the way of our professional relationship," he reassured me. "I respect you."

"I like working with you too."

"You impress me, Veronica. You have so much potential. You're a star no matter what you're asked to do. Even delicate issues, like, well, for example, Chloe. Thank you again for that."

"No problem," I replied.

"I hope she was fairly cooperative?" he inquired, his voice casual.

"No, she was completely incoherent. Don't worry, I won't tell anyone about you and Chloe." The bitter words were out of my mouth before I could stop them. I almost gasped in horror of the slip.

He paused and studied my face carefully. My expression betrayed my mistake. "What do you mean you won't tell anyone about me and Chloe?" he asked.

"No-nothing," I stuttered. "I mean I won't tell anyone about Chloe and how you asked me to send her home."

"Well, if Chloe was so incoherent, then who told you?"

I stared back at him helplessly. "Don't worry, I won't tell anyone."

"That's right, you won't tell anyone because it's absolutely untrue. Who is spreading these incriminating lies about me?"

I remained silent, deliberating over who to believe.

"Veronica, it would be a shame that all your hard work went to waste because you won't tell me who is falsely accusing me of something very serious."

The success of my Gi-Spot party seemed a distant memory now that I was teetering on the brink of failure with both of my bosses. I had worked my ass off over the last several months and had even received an illustrious invitation to visit the New York offices. I did not want all my hard work to be for nothing because of silly office gossip.

"It was Stevie," I finally said. "But he's not spreading rumours. He just told me."

"Stevie? Was he the one who hooked up with Frederico last night?"

"How did you know that?"

"Hmmm, that's what I suspected so thanks for confirming. So if you and Stevie don't spread these rumours, I won't report Stevie's indiscretions to HR," Caden smiled cooly. "Deal?"

I stared back at him, horrified. "You don't have to threaten me. I wouldn't have told anyone."

"One can't be so sure," he got up and held open his door, until I removed myself from his office.

I was ashamed that I had implicated Stevie to save my own ass. I avoided warning him about the arrangement I had formed with Caden until I could no longer bear the remorse. I prayed that he would forgive me.

I found Stevie in his office, tidying up, which was an unusual. Unusual because he was never in his office and because he never tidies up. He looked up at me coldly.

"How could you rat me out like that?"

Shit, I had not expected Caden to act so quickly in covering up his indelicacies.

"I'm sorry. He threatened me." While it seemed like the only choice when under Caden's intense interrogation, it now sounded like a pathetic excuse.

"How could you do that to a friend? I was the only one who ever helped you, even when you had no friends. I never in a million years would have expected that you, of all people, would betray me like this."

"I'm so sorry. I hope we're still friends."

"Caden told HR about Frederico. I'm fired."

"What?" I realized with dismay that Stevie was packing up his things and not tidying up his office. "He said he wouldn't say anything," I added as a weak afterthought.

"Far be it for you to trust that sleazy male slut than to trust your own friend," Stevie replied. "Your *ex*-friend. You back-stabbing bitch."

Stevie's harsh comments stung. I felt incredibly selfish. "I deserve that."

"I'm glad we agree. Now leave and don't ever talk to me again."

STEVIE DIDN'T RETURN any of my texts, emails or phone calls. I didn't stop trying. Over fear of further retaliation from Caden, I didn't tell Sydney the details. Instead, I kept to myself at Gisele and threw myself deeper into my assignments, hoping with steely determination to reverse Savannah's distrust of my office ethics. Now that I was finally convinced that a romance with Caden was an impossibility, my new obsession became my New York goal.

Devastatingly, Savannah cancelled my visit to New York until I could prove to her that I was capable of conducting myself in an appropriate manner. Almost as devastating, were it not for my recent discoveries of his questionable character, it was announced that Caden was transferring to Japan as head of Gisele Skin Care, effective immediately. The announcement stated that this promotion was a wonderful opportunity for Caden to leverage his exceptional leadership and strategic talents in launching into the lucrative Japanese skin care market. The memo went on to thank him for his many accomplishments at Gisele Canada and wish him the best in his important new role in Japan. The rumour was that he was not as particular to Japanese women as he was to young female Canadian Gisele employees, who would miss him the most.

Shortly thereafter a memo was released from HR stating that, due to the actions of certain individuals at the Gi-Spot party, alcohol will be banned from all future work functions. Office gossip was rampant and the news of Stevie's transgression quickly spread throughout Gisele like Stevie's bad imaginary rash. Unfortunately, Stevie's legacy became that of the idiot who singlehandedly outlawed alcohol from Gisele parties. It was not looked upon fondly to say the least.

Chloe was well aware that I had not been motivated by pure intentions in helping her get home safely from the Gi-Spot party and thus, it did not change her intense sense of loathing for me. The rumour soon started that I had ratted out Stevie. If it were even possible, I sunk lower in popularity as people avoided me as fervently as Stevie avoided virgin after-work beverages lest I get them fired.

Even Chloe could not escape the gossip fiends and the news of her pill-popping tendencies soon erupted, to my delight. I derived some satisfaction in overhearing Chloe vehemently and angrily defend herself at the coffee bar at any opportunity, even to those who did not appear to know her.

In comparison to the scandalous gossip at Gisele, the Heidi and Mateo coupling was boring and received little air time, except for the fact that they had been appropriately disciplined by HR for their unprofessional PDA at the Gi-Spot party. There was speculation that this had also contributed to the infamous memo, now unaffectionately dubbed the Prohibition Memo.

Having internalized Chloe's harsh criticism, Jasmine Tit had cut down significantly on the use of her boyfriend's opinion as a topic of conversation and as a result, had much less to say. It became evident that the reason she so extensively leveraged her boyfriend in conversation was that he was, in fact, much more interesting than her.

My friendship with Sydney unceremoniously ended when she found out from Stevie the true reason for his sudden departure. She immediately stopped talking to me and now looked at me with more aversion than the thought of working past 5 pm.

"How's Stevie?" I asked Sydney one day at the coffee bar as a means of potentially breaking her silence. "Has he found work?"

"He's fine," she said, avoiding my eyes and walking past me.

"Please give him my best," I called after her. She didn't respond, signaling that her silence would continue indefinitely.

The only work colleague who still spoke to me without abhorrence was Mateo. He remembered that I had honoured his request to keep his relationship with Heidi a secret and assured me that he did not believe the rumours. He told me he was my biggest defendant when people dissed me but it was tough because I had a lot of "haters".

I wanted to start fresh in a new city where I didn't know anyone, like New York. I did not find it suitable yet to discuss my progression to New York with Savannah and instead set a meeting with Oompa Loompa to gain his perspective. Granted, it was brought on by copious amounts of alcohol, but he was bursting with praise over the party that was supposed to have paved my way to New York.

As I rode the elevator up to the executive floor, I looked back at my determined and polished reflection in the elevator mirrors. I was surprised to observe how confident I seemed, despite my many "haters". I remembered my first visit to Oompa Loompa – scared, insecure and, worst of all, badly dressed. Then again, better to be badly dressed than a fashionable bitch who stabbed her best friend in the back to further her career.

"Veronica! Please, come in, come in." At least I was still held in high regard by Oompa Loompa, which I appreciated given my current circumstances, even if he was an Oompa Loompa.

"I've come to talk to you about New York," I said, not bothering to placate him with small talk.

"Ah, what about New York, my friend?"

"How am I doing? How soon will it be that I'm transferred to New York?"

Oompa Loompa chuckled, endeared by my impatience. "Well, one cannot put a timeline on such things."

I felt my resolute expression slide off my face. "You did. You said it would be two years."

"Well! That is a rough estimate. It depends."

"On what?" I asked, barely able to hide my frustration at his poor interpretation of a two year timeline.

"On opportunity, on your progression," he offered, gesturing vaguely with his hands. "The best person to talk to is Savannah. She has the most influence in these matters. Have you spoken to her about it?"

I shook my head, feeling defeated. I had wholeheartedly and naively dedicated a year of my life to an empty promise. All I was left with was an ex-gay boyfriend; a disgusted and distrustful boss; a desperate crush cut short by harsh reality (and banishment to Japan); work colleagues that wholeheartedly hated me; and no friends. Well, I did have one friend left. But there are some things that even Jager can't solve.

Chapter 21: A Hasty Decision

"SAVANNAH, CAN I BOTHER YOU for a moment?" I greeted Savannah, unannounced, at her door.

Savannah looked up from her computer, irritated. "Can you set up a meeting with my admin? I think I have some time available early next week."

"No, this will only take a moment," I entered her office, closed the door behind me and sat down. "I spoke to Oomp- I mean, Etienne, regarding New York and he told me to come see you."

"Veronica, please don't waste my time repeating conversations. I told you that your visit to New York is delayed until further notice. I'm appalled that you would go over my head and speak to HR about it, like a petulant child."

"No, not my visit to New York, my transfer to New York," I responded with a steady voice as I unabashedly looked back at her. "Etienne told me when I started that I could transfer to New York within two years."

Savannah laughed. "Well, that's outrageous. I cannot believe that Etienne would even suggest that. It's impossible for you to transfer to New York as an Assistant Manager. It would be years before we would even consider such a thing."

"Well then I quit," I responded.

Savannah looked momentarily surprised but swiftly recovered. "Quitting is a ridiculous negotiating tactic. Not to mention unprofessional. That's quite enough."

"I'm serious, Savannah, I quit. Gisele is just not for me. Thank you but I want to pursue other career opportunities."

Savannah stubbornly remained disconcerted. "You're upset and stressed right now so you don't know what you're talking about. Take a week off on my dime, come back rested, and then we'll talk."

"OK, but I'm just going to come back after a week and quit."

"I think you will come to regret this hasty decision," she assured me.

With the luxury of not having to wake up to an alarm buzzer, I slept deeply and soundly, clocking an average of twelve hours every night. I discovered how little I could get done in a day. I was able to enjoy simple things like sunlight and soap operas. My bob had grown out to shoulder length and was getting scraggly so I had the dead ends trimmed off, not at Holt Renfrew, but at a reasonably-priced salon I found walking around my neighbourhood. I wanted to grow my hair long again. I returned several over-priced items of clothing I had hastily bought to impress Caden and my colleagues at Gisele but had not yet worn. As for the other trendy and non-functional items that I had only worn once or twice, I sold them on Craigslist.

I couldn't stop thinking about Stevie and tried to control my stalker-ish apologies. I realized that he meant more to me than just a work mentor and fashion advisor. Maybe if I had valued him as the dear friend and boyfriend that he was, rather than for superficial benefits, I would have thought twice about ratting him out.

In an unusual stroke of good coincidence, Calista's PhD convocation was scheduled during my week off. I was not invited and in fact had not spoken to my girl friends in awhile, but decided it was appropriate to crash it. I hadn't attended my own convocation for my MBA because I couldn't get the time off work so it would be fun to imagine myself receiving the honour. I scanned the audience looking for Jackie and Lindsay but could not find them.

There was something very honourable and romantic about the

black gowns and caps that made me feel nostalgic. I didn't know whether I was nostalgic for the sense of youth and endless possibility that comes with graduation or for my own innocence and idealism when I graduated. I cheered loudly when Calista was awarded her diploma. I heard a boisterous whistle, which helped me locate Jackie and Lindsay. Jackie, fingers in mouth, continued to whistle enthusiastically to the chagrin of those around her until Calista returned to her seat.

After the ceremony, I watched Jackie and Lindsay run up to hug Calista. I allowed them a few moments before joining them.

"Congratulations," I told Calista. They looked shocked to see me.

"We didn't invite you because we figured you were working and you couldn't come," Lindsay jumped in, nervously.

"That's OK. I understand. Hey, big news – I quit my job! So I have a lot of spare time now."

They looked disbelievingly at me. "Well, actually, I tried to quit but my boss wouldn't let me. She told me to take a week off so I'm on vacation right now but then I'm going back and I'm definitely going to quit. Again."

They looked skeptical and uncomfortable as I continued to ramble. "I realized what a selfish bitch I was and I can't really blame Gisele but, well, I kind of do. I guess."

I did not find their silence and dubious expressions very reassuring.

"My parents are looking for me over there," Calista finally said, motioning arbitrarily. "They look lost. I'm going to go grab them. Veronica, thanks for coming. It was nice to see you."

Calista ran off, perhaps a little too quickly. I was starting to get nervous at their unenthusiastic reception. I wasn't expecting a welcome back parade but at least some favourable signs that they were happy to see me return from corporate hibernation.

"I feel horrible about what a bad friend I've been over the past year and I'm so sorry. Can you please forgive me?" I asked.

Jackie spoke up after a tense silence. "Lindsay has something to tell you about the wedding." Lindsay's eyes widened in alarm as she looked back at Jackie pleadingly. Jackie backed away. "I'm going to be at the punch bowl. I hope it's spiked."

"Oh yeah, the wedding's coming up," I turned to Lindsay. "I should be getting fitted soon for my bridesmaid gown and all that fun stuff."

"About that..." Lindsay looked at the ground.

"What?" I asked, feeling uneasy.

"I'm sorry but you were so busy all the time and you weren't keeping in touch. We could never get a hold of you. And when we did see you, all you did was talk about Stevie and your job. It was like you didn't care about us anymore. Or you thought you were too good. I didn't think I was the bridezilla type but I got nervous and asked someone else to be my bridesmaid. And now I feel bad because...you're different and it's just not the same and...I hate all this wedding drama."

I stared at her throughout her ungraceful speech, horrified. "You *un-bridesmaided* me?"

She looked back at me with a tortured expression. "Your hair looks nice." she finally said.

I did not thank her for the compliment but turned and walked away.

I RETURNED TO work, physically refreshed and ready to face the hateful glares from my colleagues and scorn from Savannah.

"How was your vacation?" Savannah asked me when I knocked on her door first thing Monday morning.

"Good," I entered and shut the door behind me. "Thanks for giving me the time off."

"I have good news for you," Savannah smiled. "I've been having discussions and making some calls regarding a possible transfer to New York. It's looking somewhat favourable that perhaps something may emerge within a year or so. Etienne should never have made such an unusual promise but then, these are unusual circumstances."

I swallowed, considering her proposal for a moment. The offer was exciting, but it did not escape me that her offer was couched in vague and uncertain terms such as "*perhaps*", "*may emerge*" and "*a year or so*".

"Thank you for the opportunity but I still resign. This is my two weeks notice." I handed her my resignation letter that I had copied from the Internet. She did not take it so I placed it politely on her desk. She looked unnerved.

"Is your dog OK?" I asked.

"Gucci's fine," she responded. "It's disappointing that you are turning down such an incredible opportunity."

"It sounds more like a possibility," I corrected her. "And not so much an opportunity."

"Well. That is more than what most people get."

"Things can change," I replied.

I excused myself wondering why Savannah had appeared so unsettled. It seemed unfathomable that it had anything to do with my resignation but then, maybe she gets evaluated on retention.

The first person I told about my resignation was Sydney. We were no longer friends but for some reason, I wanted her to hear it from me.

"So I quit," I greeted Sydney.

"Yeah, I know."

"How? I just did it a second ago." I hadn't realized that office gossip travelled by way of osmosis.

"Office pool," she shrugged. She gestured at her whiteboard. I saw that there were several names of colleagues, each paired with a date. "I won."

"Oh." I contemplated congratulating her for a moment but then realized that deriving profit out of someone else's hardship was not worthy of praise.

"I never paid Stevie for the dress he got me for the Gi-Spot party." I handed Sydney the cheque I had made out to Stevie.

Her eyes widened as she looked at the amount. "I'd just return it if I were you, that's a lot of money for a dress."

"No, I can't do that. That would be dishonest." I didn't really care about my honesty to the retailer. I was hoping that this gesture would somehow get back to and prove to Stevie that I really was a good person.

Sydney looked back at me in disbelief.

"It's a beautiful dress and it reminds me of him so I want to keep it."

"So be it." Sydney shrugged, accepted the cheque and resumed typing on her computer.

I remained at her cube, searching for eloquent words but they did not come. After several moments of silence, Sydney gave me a look of disdain that she could only have perfected from receiving countless such looks from Savannah.

"Look, I know I was totally horrible to Stevie. I have no excuse and I deserve losing him as a friend. But I just want to know if he's OK. Can you at least just let me know how he's doing?"

She reflected for a moment and then carried on at her computer.

"OK, I understand." I turned to leave, disappointed.

"No, wait, here's an email I just got from him this morning. You can read it."

> Hi – Thanks for having dinner with me last week. It was very appreciated. I have to tell you that unfortunately Marcus is straight...Those bloody Europeans play with our minds and sensibilities so much!! He just has the most adorable look, I had to restrain myself from nibbling on his ears.

I sicken myself sometimes.

Also tried my first AA meeting on Friday.

Oh my God! What a bunch of wackos. It felt like a church youth group at the local evangelical hall – no, make that Pentecostals (those are the ones that believe in talking in tongues). I'd rather just pay someone to hypnotize me sober. I always do prefer the easy way out…"

"AA? That's a little excessive. I didn't know he was an alcoholic."

"There's probably a lot of things you didn't know about him. He's going back to school and wants to be sober. He studying to be a fashion buyer."

I smiled, feeling an immense sense of pride for him. "Well…he sounds great."

"Hardly. He's an unemployed alcoholic."

"No, I mean…he sounds like himself."

Sydney shot me a look of complete disagreement. "OK."

"Thank you." I didn't ask her to give Stevie my best wishes as she probably wouldn't and he likely wouldn't much care anyway.

I dropped by Mateo's cube to let my one remaining loyalist know (and Heidi by association as she had become somewhat of a permanent fixture after the PDA incident). It gave me a sense of comfort knowing that the information came from me and not from some nasty source. They were not surprised but seemed genuine in their well wishes.

"Damn, I lost the pool," Mateo grinned. "I thought you'd last at least another couple of months."

As I turned to leave, I realized that Chloe had been standing behind me, evidently having heard everything. She was quite pleased with herself. "Poor you. Now that Stevie's gone, you finally realized that you just can't cut it here. Must suck to have everyone hate you."

"Good luck with your anger management issues," I said, unaffected by her words, and walked past her unsettled expression.

Savannah was waiting for me at my cube when I returned.

"I've been thinking about your transition plan," she said.

"In the last ten minutes?" I couldn't help myself from saying, albeit politely.

"Well, your assignment is critical. Phat Launch is scheduled to launch in two months and with very little notice it's difficult to backfill your position so I'd like you to accelerate the launch to make it happen before you leave."

I was astonished by the preposterous request. "I'm sorry but that's not reasonable…or even possible."

"Well, consider extending your resignation so that you can launch Phat Lash. It's only an extra two months and it would be a great resume builder."

Still taken back by her insistence, I was so dumbfounded that I could not find a suitable response.

"It would receive a glowing description in your reference letter," she smiled.

"I'll finish what I can in two weeks," I responded.

Savannah's expression darkened momentarily. "Well, think about it." she added with a cheerful but strained smile.

Incredulous but sheepishly triumphant, I must have sat still for several minutes, relishing Savannah's loss of power over me, now that I had quit before I could be fired. I soon heard feverish typing from my cube neighbour and remembered once again that I had a cube neighbour. I heard him laugh softly and somewhat in delight to himself. I was perturbed to hear sounds coming from his cube but then I suddenly sat up in surprise and realization. I got up slowly and silently and made myself stealthily over to his cube and stood quietly outside, watching him type over his shoulder.

My eyes narrowed in disbelief and outrage as I saw that he was typing a blog entitled Gisele Gossip. I could see the words:

```
It's official. Savannah's crazy. Why else would
she have begged Veronica to stay longer after her
much-celebrated resignation? Come on Savannah,
don't make us hate you any more than we already
do!
```

"You little bugger," I said, arms crossed.

My cube neighbour yelped and shot up a foot in the air. He fumbled to hide what he was typing as he looked over his shoulder, "Oh my God, you scared me!"

"You should be scared," I said as ominously as I could. "Gossip Girl."

He seemed to shrink in his chair, his eyes betraying his panic. His small frame looked vulnerable as his mouth opened and closed uselessly, searching for a miraculous explanation. I felt sorry for him. Someone who gains pleasure from spying on other people and starting nasty rumours must have a pretty boring and sad existence.

"Make my last entry good," I finally said once I felt I had sufficiently unsettled him with my unflinching glare. He nodded, unnerved.

I walked away, muttering, "I gotta get out of this place."

Chapter 22: Reassessment

"Cheers to Ronnie not selling her soul!"

"Or to renting it out for a year and then taking it back," Calista added to Jackie's toast. I let that one slide, as it was true and I was sucking up to my girls to win them back.

"Or to being so understanding about being unbridesmaid-ed," Lindsay said, her expression betraying her remaining sense of guilt over her decision.

I was back at our favourite pub, the Betty Ford Clinic, with Jackie, Calista and Lindsay.

"So what are you going to do now?" Calista asked.

"You know, I didn't think I would but I really like marketing so I think I'm going to check out some less…intense companies."

"Whatever happened to saving the world?" Lindsay asked.

"Well, maybe later, but for now I'm open. And besides, I don't think not-for-profit was what I really wanted. It just seemed, I don't know, honourable."

"You don't need an honourable job to be an honourable person," Calista said. I smiled at her. I missed Calista's philosophical Zen Buddhist musings.

"True. Maybe I should just focus on trying to be an honourable person."

"Don't be so hard on yourself," Lindsay said. Always the first to soften, Lindsay was the first to reach out to me after I had emailed the group a very long apology letter. I didn't know whether the gays are more bitter and apt to holding grudges than long time girlfriends but the girls were instantly receptive to my sincere – if not at the point of groveling – apology.

"Oh no, we're going to milk your guilt for as long as we can. Just you watch." Of course, Jackie would like me to grovel some more.

Jackie brought me up to date on her dating life. She had, in fact, gone on a couple dates with the drummer (aka Naked Towel Boy) of Carpenter Boy's band. At the time I was MIA, and so she hadn't taken advantage of the situation to set me up with Carpenter Boy. Alas, after a couple of dates, she found Naked Towel Boy to be a yawn, as he was only capable of talking about his band and seventies rock bands, two topics that did not particularly excite Jackie, even if he was a hot yawn.

I didn't update them on the embarrassing encounter with Caden in the church basement that had triggered my demise but I did tell them about how I had ratted out Stevie and how he had de-friended me. I didn't know whether they associated Stevie with my change in behaviour but they did not seem that devastated for me, nor did they try to hide it.

"Oh well, life goes on," Lindsay said. Jackie and Calista clinked their glasses together in approval.

Lindsay's wedding was in a couple months and while I had been unbridesmaid-ed, I was nonetheless relieved to still be invited after my obnoxious behaviour over the past year. I didn't know if things would ever get back to normal with my girl friends but at least they were giving me a chance to earn their trust back.

"Did you ever become friends with anyone else at Gisele?" Calista asked.

"No," I answered. I considered putting in a good word about Sydney but then thought it would be too complicated to explain. I was still a little upset about her abrupt decision to end our acquaintance based on Stevie's account of what happened, but then I too would be forever distrustful in that environment.

"Whatever happened to Caden?" Jackie asked.

"Banished to Japan," I laughed. Lindsay appeared physically relieved. "Turned out he was a douche."

"Well, I hope young Japanese girls don't like douches," Calista said.

Alas, I did not believe that Japanese girls would be immune to his charms. Out of curiosity, I had visited dontdatehimgirl.com and read every morbid detail about Caden. The Internet certainly isn't the binding authority on truth and can be a great venue for love-scorned women to vent vengefully. But the entries were so numerous and consistent that it was hard to deny Caden was a douche bag. Had I known the extent of his douche bag-ness, I wasn't sure it would have changed anything. I would rather reserve judgment for myself, even if my judgment has proved to be hugely inaccurate and biased by good looks.

A few days after I gave Savannah my two week's notice, I received a letter in the mail via international courier. It was a glowing reference letter from Japan. I read the contents, baffled.

"What the hell?" I said out loud when I saw that it was signed by Caden.

I kept reading it over and over in confusion until I realized there was someone watching me. My cube neighbour, aka Gossip Girl, was peering over our shared cube wall looking at me, completely oblivious to how creepy he looked.

"Did you get it?" he asked.

I looked back at him in confusion. "What do you mean?"

"The reference letter from Caden," he replied in a stage whisper.

"I don't get it. Did you forge it?"

He shook his head and continued to talk in a stage whisper. "I bribed him."

"Oh, how sweet of you."

"With his affair with Chloe. I didn't blog about it because I wanted to save it for something juicy."

"Makes sense. But how is my reference letter juicy?"

He looked around furtively. "That way you won't tell anyone about me."

"Well, I never would have anyway," I replied. Still fresh from the trauma of backstabbing Stevie, the notion of ratting out someone, even if they deserved it, made me ill. Gossip Girl looked dubious. It seemed I was way beyond the point of winning over my less-than-savoury colleagues. "But thanks, I guess."

"I'm going to miss you," he said. "As a neighbour. I get a lot of material from sitting beside you. I hope your replacement is as screwed up and loud as you are."

"Uh…thanks." I was certainly appreciative of the mutual benefit of Gossip Girl's bribe but made a mental note to warn my replacement to watch her back.

Indeed, Savannah reinforced my expendability by the speed in which she found a suitable replacement for me. The new hire made me feel old and jaded. She was a pretty little thing, fresh out of school, bright-eyed and bushy-tailed like Bambi in spring time. She was going to get skinned alive.

I was glad that I would have the opportunity to bring her on with the diligence and respect that Stevie granted me. It made my betrayal sting more when I thought back to his eagerness to help even when he barely knew me. Of the many things I learned from Stevie, he taught me that you don't have to save the world to be charitable.

"Thank you so much for all your help!" Bambi gushed to me on my last day as I sincerely wished her good luck. "I hope that I can do half as good a job as you did."

I looked at her like she was Jackie refusing a first date. "Who told you that?"

Bambi blushed. "Well, Savannah just says that I have big shoes to fill."

"Oh." I hated to admit just how proud that made me feel.

"Do you mind if I ask you why you quit?"

"It just wasn't for me." I shrugged, not wanting to bias or worry her with my experience.

"Well, I hope it's for me. I have so much to learn!" Was this how ridiculously naive and idealistic I appeared to everyone when I started?

"Let me ask you one thing," I said. Bambi leaned forward as if to receive a blessing. "New York or Paris?"

"Oh, right here," she replied without hesitation. "I'm happy right where I am. But I'm open, because, well, things always change."

"I think you'll be just fine." Bambi was smarter than I thought. "And also," I raised my voice for the sake of Gossip Girl. "There's no privacy in this cube environment so don't ever have any private or personal conversations in your cube."

"Never!" she assured me with big doe eyes. I thought I heard Gossip Girl say, "Bitch."

On my way out, I stopped my Savannah's office to say good-bye. Savannah wasn't what one would label as the sentimental type, but I was surprised that I didn't even get a card or a *nice working with you*, if not for the sincerity then for the gesture.

"Have a glass of champagne with me," she suggested.

"Right now?" I was hoping to never see her again, much less meet up for a drink with her.

She opened a desk drawer and pulled out a bottle of Veuve Clicquot and two plastic champagne glasses.

"It's my favourite," she explained in response to my raised eyebrows, as if it were a logical and appropriate response.

"Should I close the door?" I asked.

"No, we're good," she said as she smoothly and effortlessly popped the bottle.

"Well, I didn't realize you were this happy to see me go," I joked.

"I'm happy for you," she replied, handing me my glass. We clinked plastic glasses. I took a sip as Savannah downed the whole glass in one gulp. I awkwardly continued sipping.

“So, any plans?” Savannah asked, pouring herself another glass. She offered me a top-up but I politely declined.

“No, not really. I’m just going to see what’s out there and what fits me best.”

“Well, here’s a few good recruiters. If you need any references, I’m happy to be one.” She handed me a piece of paper containing a list of recruiters.

“Thanks,” I took the paper, surprised at the gesture. It was, well, nice.

“Don’t do the charity thing. It pays crap. Stick to marketing for now,” she advised.

“OK.”

“Yeah, stick to marketing,” she mused. “You’re not bad. I just hope you can find a good company that could help you, you know, get better.”

“Uh…thanks.”

“And you should get a boyfriend your own age. It will help keep you from…distractions.”

I hastily finished my glass of champagne. “Well, thanks for all your help and advice. I really learned a lot from you.”

She nodded. “Good luck.”

As I walked out of Gisele’s lobby for the last time, I noticed the life-size posters of models lining the walls and remembered how terrified they made me feel on my first day. Now they looked ridiculous to me, trapped forever inside of their contrived images. I was free.

I met Oompa Loompa coming out of the elevator, who was on his way down from the executive level to Gisele’s main level.

“You are always welcome back,” he said and kissed me on both cheeks in his usual ceremonious manner.

“Thank you,” I said, knowing that wasn’t true.

Outside, it was unexpectedly raining. I didn’t have an umbrella on me but it was a warm, light autumn rain and it was nice. I walked home at a leisurely pace, happy that the rain perhaps hid a few tears.

I wasn't sure whether they were tears of relief, joy or even sadness. But what I was sure of was that it was over.

I spent the next few weeks rebuilding my friendship with my girls, reducing the volume of my obsessive communication to Stevie, meeting recruiters and assessing available marketing jobs. Unlike my post-grad hysteria, I was in no rush and had no unreasonable restrictions, such as *must allow me to save the world* or *will only consider Amnesty International.* That, combined with having Gisele on my resume, really opened my options. I didn't yet know my life's calling but that was OK because I had my whole life to figure that one out.

During this period of reassessment, I bumped into Will at the garbage chute, of all glamourous places.

"Hey, how's your band?" I asked.

"Good, great," he responded.

"How's your gay boyfriend?" he asked as a joke.

"We broke up."

"Oh? I'm sorry." He looked vaguely confused and uncomfortable.

"Yeah, well," I shrugged.

"Well, see you around," he said as I stopped at my door. He kept walking.

I braced myself and took a deep breath.

"Hey, Will," I called. He turned around. "Does the offer still stand?"

"What? For the banana milkshake?"

"No, definitely not for the banana milkshake. To help me assemble the Ikea unit."

"That's still not assembled?" he asked.

"Yeah, I suck."

"Yeah, sure. I could do that…sometime."

"OK, well, I'll be around so just let me know," I tried to say as casually as possible.

"OK," he nodded, trying to look just as casual.

"OK," I said. We stood looking at each other, nodding so I

added, "Great."

"Yeah," he said. "So…how about tomorrow night?"

I smiled. "Perfect. I'll be right here."

As for Stevie, he never did return any of my emails. I continued to send one once a week anyway, just to let him know how I was doing in the slim chance that he still actually cared. I came to think of it as my weekly diary entry. At first I used to picture him secretly looking forward to receiving my emails but after awhile of no response, he became such a distant memory that he almost seemed imaginary. At least he was to my girls. Since they never met Stevie, they claimed he was a figment of my imagination, a mirage brought on by excessive fatigue and stress-induced insanity.

Eventually, the shame of betraying Stevie stopped gnawing at my chest, and I found myself smiling when I thought about him. Yes, I will forever remember his invaluable fashionista advice but what left a much deeper imprint in me was his generosity of spirit, his empathy for the troubled and his flair for living. That's why I love my gay ex-boyfriend. If we were to never see each other again, I will always carry these pieces of him with me.

It made me sad that Stevie may never know or see how he inspired me to be a better person and a better friend. I didn't know how much longer I would remain hopeful that Stevie would one day return my emails. But Stevie did leave some hope for me and I think it's one of the best gifts he gave me: after all the disagreeable human behaviour I encountered and perpetuated over the past year, I believed even more in the good of human nature. And that is, I must say, pretty honourable.

ACKNOWLEDGMENTS

Thank you to all my dear friends for your love, kindness, help and advice throughout this journey. I am touched by your unwavering support and belief in me.

I would be remiss not to thank my gay boyfriend from long ago, Jack Renteria, for the inspiration. We may live in different countries but I don't consider you my ex.

Thanks to Rebecca Doll for the coaching and discipline that helped me take the words out of my head and heart and make a novel out of it.

And finally, a big thanks to Michelle Halket for taking a chance on me and publishing this book.

This book belongs to

Malika DeYnes

Name

I ♡ books

A b c d e f g h l

g k l m m o p q n

s t u v w x y

Z

CPSIA information can be obtained at www.ICGtesting.com
Printed in the USA
LVOW131815151112

307507LV00011B/58/P

9 781926 760896